William McLuen

Looking Forward

William McLuen

Looking Forward

ISBN/EAN: 9783337371623

Printed in Europe, USA, Canada, Australia, Japan

Cover: Foto ©Andreas Hilbeck / pixelio.de

More available books at **www.hansebooks.com**

Looking Forward,

—OR—

Glimpse by an Observer of the past, present and probable future of our country, politically.

~~~~~~ BY ~~~~~~

WILLIAM McLUEN.

Coming Events Cast their Shadows before them.

PRICE 25 CENTS.

Sent post paid on receipt of price. Address WM. McLUEN, Perry. Iowa.

———o———

PERRY, IOWA,
CHIEF STEAM PRINTING HOUSE
1891

PREFACE.

A disposition to criticise is not generally regarded as evidence of an Angel in disguise, and this modest little pamphlet may unluckily be construed by some, as inclined to find fault with our social and business customs generally. But certainly no doubt need exist in the minds of any as to what is intended in its attempt to solve our political party problem.

The writer has no apology or excuse to offer for its style or imperfections, but lack of ability to do better, and can only expect that it will receive all the attention it may seem to deserve. The manner adopted in presenting the subject, it is hoped however, will prove sufficiently novel and interesting to accomplish in some degree the design of its publication, and help secure the attention of others more able to a consideration of our political destiny.

It may be ridiculed, or in a so-called charitable way, considered unworthy of notice by partisan interests, and many who are unfortunately as I believe, controlled too much by the party lash. But however this may be, I will trust to the sentiment of a people, who have been long enough defrauded by political buncombe, and those who prefer to follow the dictates of their own judgement for the general good, in preference to mere party strife, to indorse any and every effort in a fair way to avert a national calamity, that will as surely come as the moons nocturnal appearance to our planet, if not prevented by the prompt intelligent effort and co-operation of the laboring men of our country, and those in sympathy with them.

The number and diversity of questions, considered and discussed, and the ways and methods adopted to advertise and boom what we call business interests, and the schemes invented and practiced to get gain and fame in this fast age of sharp competition and strife, is remarkable, and if not a struggle for existence, in which the weaker go to the wall, it certainly may be considered one for financial, social and business supremacy, and one in which those who succeed are generally admired, and those who fail find little sympathy.

Nor is the average American citizen much disposed to trouble himself, as a rule, investigating, or even considering the character of vocation or causes that usually lead to such results, before bestowing his approbation or manifesting his aversion. Indeed there seems to be something inherent in most human nature that inclines to admire success, and look with cold disfavor upon failure, regardless of the character of the cause or contestants.

The energy, ability and courage that encounters and overcomes great opposition or difficulties, even in a bad cause, often elicits a feeling among the masses of humanity quite congenial to the vanity of the evil doer. But a weak vacilating effort and consequent failure, even in a good cause, is quite generally looked upon, even by those who may approve the motive, with a kind of morbid sympathy that is much more humiliating to the sensitive mind than severe censure.

The shrewd and tricky bank cashier, for example, who steals thirty or forty thousand dollars from his confiding employers, and succeeds in getting away, and in eluding pursuit and apprehension, is quite generally regarded with a feeling of awe, akin to a simile admiration. But the poor degenerate wretch known to have stolen a dollar, or even a loaf of bread, though he may have been goaded to do so by the pangs of misfortune or poverty, will generally find these flattering impulses toward him a very scarce commodity. But after all what is such a wandering and tendency of the human mind, but an evidence of the occasional inconsistency and frailty of human nature. Certainly sober thought would in this case decide that censure and merited punishment was justly due in the first case, and sympathy and prudent surveillance in the latter. And such inconsistencies can furnish an interesting topic only to the unhappy theorist whose despondent nature vainly seeks relief in brooding over human imperfections and tendency to wrong doing, and the inconsistencies thus complained of is often but the product of perverted imagination, for the admiration thus excited is not the real article. but a morbid deflection of the real impulse, that serves to show how strong and predominant a characteristic of the human mind, admiration for commendable success is. Beneath these riffles of popular whims, will generally be found a solid and enduring stratum of just, or real admiration for the ability and success that makes the world better, and lifts humanity to a higher plain, that those who are wise will prefer to consider, and find a much more rational, as well as a more pleasant and encouraging reflection. One is a faculty of the human mind, that continue to grow stronger, as mankind becomes more intelligent and appreiative.   The other is as unreal in practice as in conception.   The admiration that is real, does not only exist while the effort or success that prompt its action is predominant, but it will also rush to the rescue should defeat or misfortune befall a faithful effort in a laudable undertaking, and generously provide for those who have thus proved worthy of its exercise and protection.

But the so-called admiration excited by the prize-fighter's skill, muscle and pluck, vanishes like a shadow when he lies bleeding, prostrate and defeated under the inhuman blows of a more powerful animal.

The intelligence, enterprise, patience and pluck manifested by Cyrus W. Field in overcoming the great obstacle that confronted him in laying the Atlantic cable, and the success he achieved in that great and laudable undertaking will be forever honored and respected on earth. and in Heaven.   But the kind of intelligence, enterprise and pluck manifested by Jesse James, and the success he achieved, will be charitably erased from the record of human events. as a humiliating and shameful evidence of man's depravity.

And so we find it in all the traits of human character, deserving just, or real admiration.   Each have their bogus counterparts or morbid deflections that the freaks of fancy are liable to mistake, or accept in lieu of the genuine article, just as some may be deceived into accepting a counterfeit bank bill, or bogus coin as an equivalent for something of real value.   It may also be observed that in the range and variety of what is practically considered legitimate business in our country, we have a heterogenious anomaly of means, methods and ways, that clearly demonstrate that the inventive genius of our citizens is in a high state of development, and evidently requires the exercise of judgment in what we call business affairs generally, or in default thereof, be left to enjoy the experience that rash and negligent methods has brought to many an adventurer. For the unscrupulous vender is aware, and the well disposed should be, that in a business sense, no other country in Christendom perhaps, can show up a larger per cent of what is known as dead beats and unreliable buyers. This may seem like looking on the dark side, but we must do it, but in the belief that time will bring a remedy. And on the other hand the well disposed patron of business can safely conclude that in addition to the natural desire to succeed in any legitimate business, common to most persons, a feverish zeal and struggle for business supremacy has grown up, that under the influence of the sharp competition and strife such a scramble for gain naturally engenders, often leads to extravegant methods to obtain the end sought, that are sometimes so palpably inconsistent with facts and common sense, as to make it appear strange that any one endowed with even ordinary judgment could be thus deceived. For in addition to the many schemes concocted and carried into effect to mislead the curious and unwary, and furnish them experience in exchange for their money. There is in the general methods adopted in advertising and trying to popularize business interests, an inconsistency, extravagance and tendency to mislead, often too rediculous for serious comment. Cases are not very rare where the advertising is much more expensive than the article advertised, and of the thousands of different articles of various degrees of merit and demerit kept on sale, and the many articles prepared for sale, or got up by different parties, and all for the same purpose. Each is more or less extensively advertised as the very best and cheapest of its kind, and each is represented by a liberal number of earnest and energetic venders, who are all fully prepared to prove this to our entire satsfaction, if we will but kindly favor them with our attention. There are so many anxious aspirants for business success, continually singing this song, with occasional variations, and novel attractions that every nostrum vender and cheap John jewelry and trash racket join in the chorus, each blowing his horn, or somebody else's horn, and all intended, they say, to protect their customers and induce others to become such. This, although but a mere intimation of the many ways and methods practiced, may seem rediculous to sober thought, but it is so, and the fact that it is, is conclusive evidence that there is a sufficient number of persons, who can in this way be induced to spend their money, to make such ways and methods profitable, for otherwise they would cease to exist. Hence, the remedy is evident, educate the masses. Complaining and fault finding is, as a rule, very disagreeable, and seldom does any good. At any rate, all this and more too is nothing more than might be reasonably expected, when we consider the number and variety of the interests involved, and the natural bent of diversified human nature in what seems to be, an irrepressible struggle for supremacy, in a country where it is generally considered a free-for-all race, and where the intellectual, social and business affairs of life are comparatively unrestrained by law or custom, and one naturally affording such stimulus to trade, and as a sequence, as natural, so many victims to shrewd and unscrupulous traffic, of course it is the province of law to protect, so far as possible, citizens from the ravages of fraud, in the guise of business. But it is not done in this country, and the remedy for this neglect, must be applied when needed. It must be admitted too, that while business matters are conducted in a legitimate way, the right to a free exercise of judgment and tact must be conceded, and if through lack of such qualifications, or from other cause, any one of mature years and legally qualified is loser in their deals, they have no just cause for complaint on this score. Admission to the school of experience must be as free as any other, to accommodate those who seem to prefer it, of course it is generally an expensive one, but at worst it but relieves its pupils of that they seem disqualified to use to any better advantage. But their rights as citizens still remain, and if there is any thing in them that even experience dearly bought will bring out, the genius of our form of government furnishes every inducement possible to profit by such experience and honorably regain lost ground, and no one would seriously claim that temporary excesses in business affairs would ever endanger the rights and privileges of any class of citizens in our country.

But when we come to look over the field of politics, and find the political organs grinding out the same old tune year after year at every election, that has so long and so often deceived the confiding party voter, and still in successful use, we are not sure we can say as much. And as we investigate we are amazed at the results, and begin to think that in politics, as conducted, will be found the chief cause of such vast difference in the worldly condition of citizens. For after duly considering and admitting the fact, that some have far reaching business sagacity, tact and energy, and others lazy, indolent and shiftless, we yet wonder why it is that in a country like this, some have piled up mountains of wealth and called millionaires, and others, said to be their equals before the law, are compelled, from sheer necessity, to toil and drudge all their lives to obtain a mere subsistance, and often a very humble and dreary one at that. If however, none but the lazy, shiftless drones were thus situated, we would say, it is as good as you deserve, but still continue to wonder how any man can start in business and accumulate even one million dollars in a single lifetime in a fair and legitimate way. But when we find that many hard working, industrious citizens, who are intelligent and sensitive, are thus struggling to support themselves and families in this free and glorious country of ours, we ask why this vast and suspicious difference that is becoming so painfully evident in the worldly condition of American citizens. It certainly is not because the provisions made by our fore-fathers, for the protection and benefit of the masses, were not sufficiently wise, just and liberal. Our American Declaration of Independence, and National Constitution was all that any fair minded man could ask. Every thoughtful believer in personal liberty considered the sentiments therein contained, the very acme of human generosity and wisdom. When these principles were promulgated and successfully defended, one hundred and fourteen years ago, their brave and generous originators and defenders could reasonably expect that the oppressed poor, who had so long suffered under the iron heel of tyranny, and subjected to oppressive taxation, unjust discrimination, poverty and starvation, without means of redress, will henceforth in America have a fair chance to assert their inalienable rights, and defend their interests. Here there will be no bowing or cringing, or timid servility of humiliated manhood, or honesty in soiled garments, to aristocratic and arrogant dudes, inheriting wealth wrung by their sires from the hard earned pittance of the toiling masses. Every citizen, no matter what his station in life, if legitimate and honorable, it was reasonably expected, would have an equal right to the good things of life, with every other citizen. All shall have a say in making the laws that shall govern them, and in selecting the persons to make, interpret and execute such laws. Education will be free to all alike, and in religious matters, each can believe just as much, and just as little as they feel disposed too, and of the creed or kind that to them may seem most acceptable. Every citizen will be perfectly free to make the most of any commendable ability they may possess, in a fair and legitimate way. In short, the people will constitute the government, and those they select to administer it shall be their public servants while so doing. And while of course disposition and ability will be different, under any conditions these principles and privileges, will secure at least a competence to all who are even moderately intelligent and industrious, and effectually bar extremes of wealth and poverty. For the laboring classes will always constitute a majority, and having the power in their own hands, they will surely effectually check any tendency to great wealth. This may be considered certainly as but a reasonable anticipation of results, when our government was founded. And now in the year 1890, after one hundred and fourteen years has elapsed since these privileges were promulgated, successfully defended and transmitted to us, it would certainly be a considerate and fair question to ask, what has been, or is now the result of these wise and generous provisions on citizens in the humbler walks of life, and for whose protection and benefit they were chiefly intended? Have results been, or are they now such as might then have been reasonably expected. and if not, why not? Who will answer.

There is a beautiful legend connected with Mohammedan faith, that to some might serve as a reminder in answering these questions. It represents justice as a strong and firm man standing upon a rock, solid and enduring. An Angel stands upon his right shoulder, representing truth with the book of life. And on his left shoulder, another Angel, representing mercy. When therefore a follower of the prophet is guilty of neglect of duty to his family, his religion or his country's interests, Justice sternly commands the Angel on his right shoulder to write it down, and the Angel on his left shoulder weeps. Or if it is true, as many good people believe, that the spirits of departed friends are hovering around us in times of difficulty and danger, powerless to help us, but anxiously watching our every act, and rejoicing when we become vigilant and strong in defence of justice, and downcast and sorrowful when we act in a deceitful or sinister way with our fellow men, what are we to suppose would be the feelings of some of our revolutionary patriots, who labored so long and so faithfully to secure to us these privileges, and were thus enabled now to witness the trickery and scheming in one State or Congressional Political Convention and Halls of Legislation, or the schemes of fraud under the sanction of legislation, instituted by rings, trusts, monopolies and other combinations, to rob the toiling masses, and then witness the patient submission of their victims. And now in order to make this matter as plain as we can, we will ask permission to go a little farther and observe that these spirits of departed friends, as many people also believe and say they have witnessed, also appear in the flesh at times, just as they were while living here, and are thus enabled under certain conditions to advise and direct, when necessary, those in whose welfare they take especial interest, and who are yet dwellers on this mundane sphere. Now let us suppose for the sake of illustration, that a few of our revolutionary patriots who helped originate and signed our Declaration of Independence, and then pledged all their earthly possessions, their honor and their lives to stand by the principles there laid down, and to make this pledge good, voluntarily exposed themselves to the most depressing hardships, suffering and danger for six dreary years for our protection and benefit, were now permitted, to be in this way, sent here from another sphere, as a committee of observation and investigation, to ascertain and report as to what, as a nation, we have done since their time to protect, preserve and defend the rights and privileges they then transmitted to us. We will say this is made known and their coming is announced. what a bustle there would be, the plain and unpretending nature of the old veterans will soon have an experience they little dreamed of in their day. Their natural aversion to aristocratic and arrogant pomp must soon undergo a severe test, and their cherished hope and expectations of the deliverance of the masses from legalized injustice and oppression is doomed to sad disappointment. But in the meantime, extensive and hurried preparations are made for their reception? They are met on their arrival, by the President and all the national dignitaries, rich capitalists and merchant princes, as they are called by adulation, railroad magnates and those of other rich corporations, and millionaires, are all there in gor-. geous array to greet and receive them. The President, in behalf of the citizens of these United States, tenders them a hearty welcome. Members of his cabinet, senators, congressmen and their high toned, aristocratic friends and acquaintances, are all profuse in their expressions of delight, at being thus enabled to see the men of whom they had read so much, and so sincerely admired. All the elite of aristocratic and fashionable dudes have richly cushioned seats, to hear and admire all this eloquent flattery. The somewhat bewildered veterans of '76, are now escorted to the national capital, as the guests of the President, and introduction after introduction is anxiously sought after by the gorgeous throng, and each has his piece of flattery prepared. The Press and the Forum vie with each other in extolling the virtues and heroism of our distinguished visitors. Devout prayers are offered up and anthems of praise sung for them in all the fashionable churches. Feasts, flattery and ceremony follow in constant succession, and all the large cities are sending their wealthy and official splendor with the most urgent invitations for the old patriots to visit them. But amid all the feasting, pompous flattery and display, the old patriots of '76 are evidently not happy.

This is noticed and talked of, and the cause charitably assigned to their rural proclivities, and lack of culture. But these conclusions begin to seem somewhat doubtful, when on receiving a very polite invitation from a millionaire to attend a banquet. The stern old chairman of the committee sends this startling reply: We must be excused, we cannot attend your banquent, we are heartily tired of all this confusion and extravagant vanity, and must now insist on being let alone, so that we can attend to the business we were sent to look after. This was a cooler and had the desired effect, and the old patriots are now getting down to work. Faithful assistants have been selected in all the states and cities. Reports begin to come in, and they are astonished to find that the population of our country has increased from 3,000,000 to nearly 63,000,000 of people, or 21 persons to every 1 in their time. Their astonishment increases when they learn the enormous increase in natural and acquired wealth, and the many wonderful improvements in what was supposed to be science, the arts, mechanics and agriculture, and in all that is supposed to relieve human toil, and add to the comfort and conveniencies of life. The railroads, the telegraph, the telephone, elec-

tric lights, electric motors, automatic machinery and the vast products
of the great west is all reported, and their astonishment has become be-
wildering. But they at once commence to make out and arrange their
report, and gradually their bewilderment gives way to a feeling of ex-
uberant joy at the wonderful growth and prosperity of our country.
And when it is supposed their work is nearly completed, invitation after
invitation is recieved from national dignitaries, rich corporations and
millionaires, entreating them to favor them with their presence. at a
grand banquet, to be given in their honor, before their departure. And
after talking the matter over, the old patriots concluded that although
not to their liking, they would have to accept some of the invitations.
But said one. citizens of our country have grown so rich and proud, I do
not feel at home among them. Yes said another, such extravagant display of wealth and pomp seems to me entirely out of place in our
country. And it is contaminating and dangerous to the perpetuity of
our free institutions. It would be, replied the old chairman, if the
wealth was not so evenly divided, but they all seem to be rich. But
even then if it prompts them to act so much like the abominable aristocrats of Europe, the rising generation ought to be taught to despise such
arrogant pomp. And how under heavens any of them ever succeed in
accumulating even one half million dollars by dint of honest effort or
fair, legitimate business is more than I can understand. And yet I
find some are estimated to be worth from $10,000,000 to $100,000,000.
But our country will never be in safe hands while millionaires are al-
lowed to grow to such extremes. For where one extreme exists, it is
very liable to produce the other in time. And when we go to this pompous spludge they call a banquet, it will seem to me like aping and trying to imitate the very practices we abhorred and rebelled against in '76.
A magnificent outfit now arrives to convey them to the banquet. Here
they come said the old chairman, and the biggest spludge of all. They
reluctantly consent to be waited on and helped to a seat in the carriage.
When they arrive, another such ordeal still more pompous has to be en-
dured. And as they are conducted into the grand apartments they are
bewildered at the dazzling display of wealth and luxury. Complimen-
tary addresses. toasts and flattering responses follow the gorgeous repast.
and finally the committee are called upon, and expected to express their
approbation. The old chairman reluctantly arose. and in a firm,
earnest way said: I dislike to take part in any exercises when I am
not in sympathy with the proceedings or customs. And I cannot say that
I am, here. I would much prefer to say something more pleasant for
you, if I could consistently do so. But I cannot afford to smother my
own convictions of duty, however anxious I may be to please you.
Such gorgeous displays of wealth and fashion I am not accustomed to
seeing. nor do I admire such as some do. We have said in our report
however. that the vast growth and unheard of wealth of our country

and citizens, for a time completely bewildered us with astonishment. And now with a hope that you will all act sensible, and not allow prosperity to make you vain and arrogant, we will at the close of this meeting bid you farewell, and return with our report to those who sent us here. These candid and sensible remarks were not very favorably recieved, and was attributed to the old man's crude nature, and all went on as before. The festivities were finally about to conclude with some brilliant display, when all at once a sensation was caused by a very plainly dressed, though a sedate and sensible looking man walking up to the closely observed chairman of the committee, who had thus addressed them. And in a very informal and plain, common sense way asked him for his attention. This brought a scornful titter from most of the gorgeous assembly. And this man, we will call him observer, was looked upon as an undignified and rude intruder. But the committee were differently impressed. The firm bearing, and flashing eye of the stranger, revealed to the old patriots something that reminded them of old Faneuil Hall in days of yore. And the mountebanks and dudes of the fashionable throng felt mortified, when they seen that the old veterans of '76 were much more anxious to talk with the stranger than with them. But the old man had no apology to offer, and at once announced his intention of seeing the stranger in a private apartment. And as they retired for the purpose, it required the efforts of all the more considerate in the assembly to suppress the intended hiss. When they reached their room the old chairman grasped observer by the hand, and in the most sincere and fervent manner addressed him thus. My friend we are glad you have come. You are the first real and natural looking American I have had the pleasure of seeing since our arrival. And such you surely must be. We have been feasted, toasted and tortured by these nabobs, until our weariness and disappointment has become depressing. Hence, I repeat I am glad you have come. For we long for congenial fellowship, and now pray tell us who you are, where you have come from, and what you desire, Observer paused and replied; I am an American citizen. I have come from the west, and I desire that you should return to our country's tried and truest friends, with a true report of the condition of the masses of our people in this country. And not with the delusion and erroneous impression you have obtained in the lap of luxury and illegitimate wealth. Just what we want responded the patriots in unison, go on. Observer continued: These gorgeous displays you have witnessed is a spludge of those, who are Americans only in name. And most of the means used to bolster them up, have been rung by extortion and class legislation, from the toiling masses and unfortunate poor. A burst of indignant resentment on the part of the patriots follows this statement, and the eyes of the old chairman flash like a meteor, as he interrupts Observer by saying in an excited manner: Excuse me my friend, can it be possible that · such humiliating conditions can exist in our country. Observer again paused to control his feelings, and then in subdued, but firm tones, said: My friends, America is to-day a country of millionaires and mendicants of vast wealth and extreme poverty, of oppressive laws and burdensome taxation, of unjust discrimination, of rings, of trusts, of monopolies, of many unfaithful public servants who make and execute laws solely in the interest of these rich nabobs, who have been entertaining you, and others like them, and seem to think and act as though the laboring man, or farmer in poor circumstances had no rights worthy of their respect or attention. After this declaration, a feeling of sorrow, mingled with disappointment and indignation, is plainly visible on the countenance of the old patriots. And Observer is so affected thereby, that he stops to contemplate in silence what is too affecting for utterance. After a few moments silence, Observer adds: You have been feasted in the mansions of the opulent, the millionaires, the railroad magnates and other rich corporations. The heads and various branches of pamp ered aristocrats, and political pets have shown you one side of this picture, in a way you admit has dazzled and bewildered you with its lavish splendor. I now ask the privilege of showing you the other side, just as it is, and then you can form your own conclusions. Just what we came for, and just what we want responded the old patriot. And sorrowful and disheartening as your statements are, if such is the case, we want to know it from personal observation, and we beg of you to assist us in obtaining facts in this way. Just the opportunity I desire said Observer. He then takes the committe to the west. They arrive when the sun is shining low in the western horizon, on a clear, cold day in November. Here said Observer, pointing to the vast area around them, mostly in corn fields. Here is naturally the most fertile country in America. It is occupied by a people that will compare favorably with any others I know of in a like avocation, for physical vigor, intelligence and industry. But they are generally in poor circumstances, and some of them, at times, hardly able to procure the necessaries of life. The old patriot looked confused, and as though he was trying to conceal a feeling of doubt. As to the truth of this statement, the country is evidently a fine and productive one said he. But I cannot understand, how the high taxes and political corruption you speak of, could be oppressive enough, or mean enough to keep such people as you describe from being comfortably situated in so fine a country and be tolerated or born by any who are worthy being considered Americans. Well · I mean to be truthful with you said Observer, but unfortunate experience

may tend to warp my judgment. But as you prefer to observe for
yourselves you will not be confined to accepting my statements. Excuse
me my friend, I do not mean to doubt your statements. But such conditions are so shamefully different from any thing we had reason to expect, that I cannot help but doubt any statement of proof short of posi-
tive evidence. Well I take that into consideration, said Observer, and I
will give you an opportunity to see for yourself. We will stop awhile
with the tillers of this fertile soil, and see hew they live, and hear what
they have to say. It is now dusk and Observer points to a farm house
close by. Here is a farmer's house, said he, who seems to be a full average in comfort and circumstances. We will stop with him to-night.
They suit the action to the words, and start for the house. As they approach the humble cottage they observe two or three half clad children
apparently shivering with cold, carrying water, procuring fuel &c., to
snpply the wants of the family. A look of troubled surprise is plainly
evident on the old patriot's face. They enter the house and find these
children's mother busy preparing a frugal supper for her family, after
having worked hard all day, at the sewing machine and wash tub, as
she afterwards told them. She greets them kindly, though timidly, as
they enter her humble home, and seems confused and humiliated for
want of means to provide each with even a rude seat, and apologised
as best she could for not having her household affairs in a more inviting
condition. This poor woman had been brought up in a more pleasant
and comfortable home. But this fact only added to the sting of humiliation in her present condition. The veterans of '76, exchange significant glances, but make every effort in their power to appear sociable and
contented to relieve the woman's embarassment. And Observer seemed
perfectly at home, and kept up a conversation with the housewife about
their social, domestic and business relations. Aiming thereby to obtain
all the information he could for his companions, and to which they lis-
tened with close attention and evident surprise. Finally after listening
to the woman's answers to Observer's questions, as to how hard they
worked, how much they raised and how little they got for it, the high
taxes and high interest on their mortgaged home, and the high prices,
because a heavy tax called protection was added, they had to pay for
most of their necessaries, the old patriot could not retain his feelings
longer, and abruptly broke out with the inqury: Madame, where is
your husband? He is out in the field husking corn sir, she meekly replied. It is nearly dark and he will soon be in with his last load, for to-
day. There he comes now, just drove up to the crib. The committee
and Observer on being thus informed, all arise and propose a talk with
him. This affords the poor woman relief, by giving her a chance to

straighten things up while they are out. As they approach her husband
the usual greeting takes place, and they soon observe that he too is clad
in cheap and ragged clothes, and apparrently shivering with cold. They
question him about the extent and quality of his crops &c., and he
answers promptly, but seems to be wondering what they have come for.
Observer tries to make him feel at ease, but he, realizing what had yet
to be done, was rather disinclined to continue the conversation, and
asked them to go in out of the cold, that he had yet to attend to his
team, feed the hogs, milk the cows and do the rest of the chores, and
then they would have some supper. After they started for the house,
and all was still, the old patriot suddenly ejaculated. My God! this
poor man works all day and half the night. Our country sure enough
seems given to extremes. Well yes, replied Observer, · laconically, you
will find rather a different state of affairs here, from what you did
among the big bugs I found you with in Washington. Yes, yes replied the old patriot, I was surprised there at the splendor and lavish
display of wealth. And here, I am still more surprised and disheartened
too at the evidence I have already had of hardship and penury. Can
it be possible that this man is an American? He undoubtedly is. replied Observer, and just about in the average condition of farmers and
workingmen of the west generally. Well, sighed the old patriot. if relief cannot be obtained, and speedily, it will be a source of regret to me.
to have found it out. When they reach the house, they find the woman,
(we will call her Mary) has ransacked every part of her abode to provide the best she had for the comfort of her guests. After a while her
husband (we will call him John) comes in, apparently worn out with
fatigue, and exposure to the cold winds of the western prairies. Supper
is announced, and after a hasty preparation, during which, John apologised by saying he dassent wet his hands, it made them crack worse.
They are soon seated around a very plain, though neat and well ar-
ranged table. And it soon becomes evident that John is a religious
man, and with him and Mary they bow their heads. and he offers up
the following petition: Lord, we thank Thee for the many blessings
with which Thou hast favored us. Bless this food to the nourishment
of our decaying bodies. and when we are done with the enjoyments and
pleasures of this life, take us to Thyself, and Thine shall be all the
praise &c.. The ludicrous contrast between poor John's real condition
in life, and the way he alluded too it in his supplications, was evidently
not in accord with the old patriot's ideas of man's duty to himself or
his Creator. And Observer was required to make all the effort he could
master to keep from violating the rules of propriety, on noticing the expression on his face at the close of the benediction. And after supper
while John was out looking after his stock, the old patriot in a musing
way remarked: This poor man is surely not sensible of his real condi-

tion in life, when he talks to the almighty about his enjoyments and pleasures, the way he seems to live. Well not exactly that perhaps, replied Observer. It is I think more the result of outside conditions. You see he has been duped and deceived by wily politicians, until he has given up all hope of earthly relief. And about the time he does so, the preacher comes along and tells him that he must thank God regularly if he is even permitted to live, as he does. And that if they attend their meetings regularly, and contribute liberally, they will live in the fine mansions in the world to come, and the other fellows will be left out in the cold. The old patriot shook his head and said: A man who could make no better showing with the chances we gave him here, would, he feared, stand a slim chance anywhere else. And a man who does not provide for his own family is worse than an infidel. John now comes in and the old man addresses him as follows: Though a stranger to you my friend, I feel a deep interest in your welfare. I trust therefore you will pardon the liberty I am about to take, of asking you some questions. , Certainly said John, evidently pleased with the stranger's sincerity and manners. You are doubtless acquainted with the rights and privileges guaranteed to citizens of our country, are you not, asked the patriot. Well, replied John, somewhat confused, all us farmers and working men think we are, but I am a little afraid to say yes, and I don't just feel like saying no. We have a book here in the house that has the constitution in it, and I have heard the Declaration of Independence read on the 4th of July, and we go to the poles and vote, and call it a free country. But of late years it seems more like talk than reality.

Why my dear friend, replied the patriot, the right to vote is the most precious and sacred right of citizenship. And if vigilantly and intelligently used will always enable you farmers and workingmen to maintain your rights and defend your interests. But neglect to use it thus, or abuse such a privilege, and all that has been done for you is practically lost, and you will, slowly it may be, but surely drift down to a level but little above the down trodden poor of Europe. John now looks downcast and the tears glisten in Mary's eyes. Observer and the rest of the committee exchange glances. And the earnest penetrating eyes of the patriot is impatiently waiting for a reply. Finally John raises his head and after a sorrowful glance at his wife and half clad children, replies in subdued tones: Well it looks some that way now, and I don't see any help for it. You don't see any help for it, repeated the patriot in thunder tones. O my friend, how inconsiderate and ungrateful that sounds to me. You don't see any help for it. Why the poor man's vote counts just as much as the rich man's. And farmers and laboring men out number the rich nabobs you say are oppressing you, more than fifty to one. Well I guess we do meekly replied John. Thunderation then what are you here for, exclaimed the old patriot, to submit tamely to any imposition or fraud that may be imposed upon you by those who at best are but your equals before the law, and rough it through life in this menial condition, when you have not only the natural right, but the legal and constitutional right as well to resist and overcome such abuses. Well I suppose we have such rights, said John, but I guess we don't know how to use them. And we can hardly tell any more who to believe. We have political parties called Republicans, Democrats, Greenbackers, Prohibitionists and God knows how many more, and some of us work and vote for one of these parties and some with another. Ah yes! then you are divided in political sentiment and action. Yes sir, said John. Well have you ever been able to discover any real difference in the character, ability and devotion to your interests in the men these parties select to make and execute your laws. Well I can't say that I have, said John. They all tell us that theirs is the true and correct doctrine, and that their sympathys is with us, and that as long as we vote their ticket we will be all right, and that they will soon bring us relief, and so on. But after they are elected, the excitement is all over, and we seldom hear any more from them until the next political campaign, when their terms are about to expire, then they come around and tell us how much they, and the party have done for us. And they tell us funny stories, and we laugh and applaud them, and if their re-election is doubtful the managers of the campaign get up political rallies and barbecues and torch light processions to enthuse the luke warm. But the relief any of them promised us has never come that I know of But I do know times are getting mighty hard, and it seems as though we can't work hard enough to keep out of debt, and live mighty saving too. Well, said the old patriot with a sigh, I feel despondent, humiliated and grieved to find the working men of our country in such a condition. And why it is that you submit to be thus defrauded, and that there are others unscrupulous and mean enough to perpetrate such swindles I can hardly reach a satisfactory conclusion. Little did we think it would ever come to this, with the country we labored so long and so faithfully to make the refuge of the poor man, where he could be free from unjust encroachments. And as to what, or whether any thing can be done to remedy this great misfortune, I am unable to say now. Mary, although very much interested, now ventured to remark that it was getting late, and all concluded to retire. John however, in accordance with his cherished custom, began making preparations for his devotional exercises. Saying to his visitors that they could remain or retire, as they wished. They thanked him and all concluded to remain. And in the short supplications, petitions were offered up, identical to those at the supper table. Unfortunately the old patriot was not just in

the right mood to relish what seemed to him inappropriate and thought-
less appeals to the most High. And the solemnity of the occasion could
not overcome his inherent desire to have matters as he thought they
should be. And they had not more than risen from their knees, when
he accosted John thus: My friend I am a believer in religion and religious liberty, and have in my weak way been instrumental in securing
to my fellow citizens the free exercise of this right. And I like to hear
supplications to the most High consistent with truth, and you I have no
doubt mean to be so. But I feel curious to know what you consider
your pleasures and enjoyments in this life, the way you are situated and
treated by the powers that be. O well, replied John with an air of of-
fended dignity, we are having a pretty tough time now, but we
hope it will be better after awhile. Ah my friend that won't do
When you make a well directed and intelligent effort you have reasonable grounds for hope, but not otherwise. Tell the Lord that you have
been a very poor and careless custodian of the liberty and privileges be-
stowed on you by your over-indulgent forefathers, and I think he will
believe you. And then resolve that henceforth as long as you are able,
that you will exert yourself in every fair and honorable way to regain
lost privileges. And my word for it, he is ready to help you, as he did
us of old. John did not seem to have any particular relish for this lec-
ture. But the earnest fervor of the patriot completely subdued in him
any feeling of resentment, and Mary made a happy diversion on the
rather awkward condition of affairs by telling how much she was interested, and that she could sit up all night and listen to the stranger.
Thank you madam, said the old man with evident relief. The clock
now struck twelve, which again reminded them of the necessity of re-
tiring, and after some pleasant remarks and a hearty good-night, all retired to rest. But John and Mary were so impressed with the stranger's
manner and talk, the inclination to sleep had left them, and each was
waiting to see what the other had to say. Mary first broke the silence
by saying: John there is something in that man's appearance and talk
that inspires confidence, and makes the future look more hopeful, don't
you think so? Blamed if there aint said John, some how or other he can
say what he pleases to me and I don't feel like getting mad at him.
What do you think they come for, John? asked Mary. Dogged if I
know said John. When I first seen them I thought maybe they come to
collect the pay for that doggoned threshing machine or twine binder, or
to foreclose that devilish mortgage. But I don't think so now. It looks
as though the old man and his companions had come to help us out in
some way. He don't seem to take much stock in your blessing and
prayer, does he John. O, I don't know, said John feigning tired.
Well. don't you think he is about right John. O, let us quit talking now

said John, I feel tired and sleepy. Well I will tell you what is a God's fact John, persisted Mary, when you joined meeting last winter, it sounded to me just about the way it does to him now. But I believe we have both got used to it, and don't notice how silly it does sound. There there, that will do, muttered John, don't bother me any more, I want to go to sleep and get up early for breakfast. Yes, and that reminds me of something else, Mary again put in, what on earth will we have for breakfast, we are out of sugar and coffee. You will have to go over to Smith's early in the morning and borrow some, until we can go to town. O. for God's sake let me rest, growled John, or I might as well get up and go now. This ended the conversation, and both sank into the arms of morphia.

When Observer and the committee awake from their slumbers, the sun is lighting up the eastern horizon, and Mary is busy preparing breakfast. All arose and dressed, and as they pass into the other room, each is greeted with a pleasant good morning sir, by Mary. After the usual preparations, all are seated, and as Mary glides here and there with apparrently a light heart and merry air to supply the table. The old patriot remarked in a low tone that it was a pity that such a woman was tied for life to a man who seemed disqualified to furnish her a comfortable home and better opportunities. John who has been out attending his stock, now comes in, and after the usual salutaticn, is seated. And as the time for breakfast approaches, he does not seem disposed to undertake his usual devotional exercises, after the raking he got from the old patriot and Mary the evening before. But their visitor's nature was more given to earnest effort than to levity on such occasions, and he came to John's relief in a plain and sensible talk. But which, however well intended, made it still more plain that John's embarrasment was noticed. And the mischievous twinkle in Mary's eye, who knew that poor John had the same identical prayer to offer up on all occasions, got matters in a shape that would hardly be deemed favorable as a stimulus to devotional supplications. After breakfast the old patriot addressed John thus: My friend you doubtless want to know who we are, and what our business is by this time, and right you should· We have come sir to observe and investigate the circumstances and condition in life of you farmers and workingmen generally, with a view of trying to ascertain the cause and correcting any abuses of power that might exist to your prejudice. I have been told that your condition and circumstances is about a fair average of your fellow citizens in a like av ocation. Is my information in your opinion correct? Well, said John after a pause, I guess I am just about in the same fix as most of the farmers in these parts, and I guess those around here are just about like they are all over. And I suppose I am just about an average of those who own the farms they live on. Some are a little better off than I am, and once in a while one who is out of debt and pretty well fixed. But there is many not so well off as I am, and there is many who are only renters, and have no home of any kind they can call their own. And American citizens? asked the old patriot. Y-e-s replied John I suppose they are. They vote, and go to all the stump speeches and rallies, and argue and quarrel over politics just like the rest of us, and I don't know but more. By this time the expression on the old patriot's face was beginning to amuse Observer again. Do you own this little farm you live on? asked the patriot. Well, y-e-s replied John, but I had to mortgage it three years ago to get $1,000 I needed to fix up, and pay some debts in town. But only got $925.00, they charged me $75.00 for commission and making out the papers. But I have to pay interest every six months on the full $1000. O, well then replied his visitor, you don't own it. You own but an equity. The fellow you got the money of has $1000.00 share in it, and much the best share. For his is steadily growing, without effort or attention. But your share requires both, and liable to lose it even then. His is sure to come, if it takes it all. While your's, if I may judge from the progress you seem to be making, is very doubtful. What do you consider the farm worth? Well, about $2500.00 said John. Then, continued the old patriot, you pay tax on three fifths and he on two fifths the valuation? No sir, replied John, I have to pay tax on all, just the same as though I owned it clear of incumbrance. And they are so high it begins to seem like paying rent. What! said the old patriot, are you sure you are giving me facts? Yes sir. said John, that's the way we have to do. O well, it is useless to ask any more questions with a view of finding out the cause of your poverty. Go on, said Observer to John, and tell him about prices you get, and those you have to pay. John said corn and oats were his chief crops, and that 16 to 18 cents per bushel was all he had been getting for either, after hauling them five or six miles. And other things we raise in proportion. But this year, for the first time for years, corn and oats will bring nearly double the old price. From what cause? asked his visitor. We have had a general failure in these crops, said John, and many producers will be compelled to buy for their own consumption. O well then, said the patriot: Politics, legislation, or traffic had nothing to do with this. It was owing to causes beyond their control, or purely accidental. Yes sir. said John, we have found that out. And we know from experience that just as soon as the least surplus is raised, the speculators will put the value down to old prices. Well, I am glad you have learned even that much, replied his visitor. For otherwise these occasional fair prices for your products, might tend to throw you still more off your guard. Yes sir, replied John, the Republican stump speakers and writers claim all the credit now for the prices we are getting.   And when it gets down to 15 and 16 cents again, they will call it over production.   John then, at Observer's request, gave the prices he had to pay for necessaries, and for professional services of all kinds the demand supports, and for incidental expenses in the way of religious, benevolent and charitable contributions, and an occasional investment to educate the heathen, besides trying to supply the needs of his own family. O Great Heavens! That's enough, said the old patriot. Many of these are worthy objects no doubt.   But with your meagre income, no wonder you are poor. No wonder this poor woman you call your wife, was ebmarrased, as I know she was, at the poverty of your home on our arrival, No wonder your poor children are running around half clad.   Well, it aint any wonder, poor John replied in subdued tones.   It seems as though we can't work hard enough to keep up even the necessaries of life, and pay interest and taxes, to say nothing about the principle and other debts I will be expected to meet. You have still other claims to meet, besides those mentioned it seemes, carelessly observed his visitor. Y-e-s, said John I owe about $75.00 on a twine binder, and about $50.00 of a doctor bill, and about $20.00 on a sulky plow, and I agreed to pay the preacher $20.00 for this year.   And he was here yesterday, and I had no money, and he wanted a fresh cow I have, and I was willing to let her go, but Mary objected and said we needed the cow too much ourselves.   And he didn't like it, and told her Saint Paul said women should obey their husbands.   And Mary is pretty saucy sometimes, and told him we could get along without his preaching better than without the milk.   And I hated it.   O, they all want their pay, and I suppose it's right they should have it. But it seems like we can't work hard enough to pay them all, and live as saving as we can.   Well, now let me tell you my friend, said the old patriot straightening up. Your evidence corroborates Observer's, only if anything it is worse than he represented, I have told you what we were here for.   I will now tell you that we had previously been through the east, and obtained a still more thorough knowledge of conditions there.   We visited your President, Senators and Congressmen, seen and talked with, all your national dignitaries, millionaires, rail road magnates, corporations of immense wealth, rich merchants and manufacturers, rings, trusts, monopolies and God knows what all we didn't see that must exist as accompaniments to many of these self evident frauds.   And we have now a sufficiently clear conception of conditions and causes, and the way our once free and happy country is tending. to make a full and comprehensive report to those who sent us.   But it will be a startling and painfully ominous one to them, as well as to us.

And what the result will finally be, I can hardly conjecture now. We leave you with sorrow and reluctance, and with no very pleasant forebodings of the future, for I fear we have come too late. And especially do we feel sorry for your poor wife, and God knows how many others no better off. And these poor children happy in their innocense and childish glee, but little knowing what the future of our country, dark as it seems to us, may have in store for them. Tears were now visible in the eyes of all. And poor Mary unable to restrain her feelings, wept bitterly, and implored the old patricts to stay and help them provide for their children. Adding. with sobs, that she would be willing to rough it through, and work hard all her life, if she only knew that her poor children would have a better chance. God bless you my dear woman, exclaimed the old patriot, but little less affected with grief, such sentiments of self denial and parental affection, helped us to gain our rights, and with God's help it may yet enable us to perpetuate them. Your devotion and example affords me encouragement. Poor John who is but little less affected, also entreats the strangers to stay, saying that he had told about them at Smith's that morning, and several were coming to see them. As he spoke, some five or six other farmers ar rived and were introduced. One of them an earnest and intelligent looking man, requested a hearing. This being freely granted. He said: My friends I know not who you are, or from whence you have come. But we have heard of you in a way that revives a hope for our country. Your presence here, and remarkable statements is in part known throughout the neighborhood. All are extremely anxious to see and hear you before you depart. And we want to call a meeting at our school house this evening. And beg of you to talk to us there publicly. Well my friend, replied the patriot, that would rather be inconsistent with our original intentions of going through the country quietly, so we could the better see things just as they are. But I am happy to say that I have had encouragement right here with this family, in the last hour, that makes me feel like doing any thing I can for you, and in any way consistent with justice. I will remain and come, but do not expect much. For I am not a fine talker, and may say some things that may not be just what you want. It matters not, replied the farmer: We want to hear a man who knows what is wrong, and will say just what he thinks, no matter whose head the hat may fit. And thanking him they started on their way, to make preparations for the meeting. During the day the committee separated. Two going to other fields of labor. The old chairman and Observer only remaining. And they were industriously engaged in collecting all the information possible about the fraud and corruption in politics. and the primal and subsequent results thereof on the confiding and misguided party voter and his interests. After supper there was evidence of a full attendance, and some enthusiastic farmers drove up with a fancy outfit decorated with flags and emblems, to convey the old man to the school house one mile distant. But to their surprise and disappointment, the old patriot objected to being thus paraded. We will walk gentlemen, said he. When the necessaries of life and a reasonable competence is maintained, it will be time enough for such display. And I don't care much about it any way. And they did walk. When they reached the place of meeting, all eyes were upon them. And a Mr. Egotism and Mr. Self-conceit came to meet them, and at once introduced themselves as residents of the country for over twenty years. They told the old man that they were thoroughly posted on the political out-look there, and each alluded to the strong influence the other could exercise over the farmers, and how they could change results of an election at will whenever they wished, that voters all came to them for advice, and—Here the old patriot called a halt, by saying with a severe and stern look: Neither of you fellows impress me favorably. You are political schemers, of small caliber no doubt, but none the less so in fact. And as such, your acquaintance or attention is not desired. This was a cooler, and Egotism and Self-conceit now turn their attention to circulating the report that the stranger who was going to address them was nothing but an old crank. And of course many believed it. Hence when he took his seat, the feeling toward him, except the few who knew him better, was not favorable. The old man realized this, but waited patiently. The meeting was finally called to order, and Egotism elected chairman. He pompously walked forward, and introduced the speaker thus: Ladies and gentlemen, we will have the pleasure of listening to an address this evening, on the political issues of the day, by a gentleman who is an entire stranger to me. I do not even know what his name or politics is, (laughter) but I hope he will prove to be sound, and that we will have a good time. After thus expressing himself with an air and expression of scorn for the speaker, he took his seat as chairman, evidently pleased with himself, and admired by many of his friends in the audience, who expected lots of fun. How their anticipations were realized, we will see further on.

After the momentary bustle caused by Egotism's flourishes, all eyes were again directed toward the speaker and Observer setting on his right. The old patriot seemed unmoved, and slowly rising he stepped to the edge of the platform and looked over the audience with a kind of indignant sympathy, that, as was afterwards told, was more than a match for Egotism's flippant remarks, and seemed to secure the respectful attention of the audience before he uttered a word. He commenced in a slow, firm voice, and said that he was not there for the purpose of talking to Republicans or Democrats, or any other political, religious, benevolent or social organization. I want to talk to you, said he, as American citizens if you can yet justly claim to be such. Nor do I feel disposed to make the least effort solely for the purpose of gaining your applause, unless you enjoy being scolded, which is not very likely. We have chosen to conceal our identity, as we want to see matters and things just as they are so far as we can, and in a quiet and unobtrusive way, with as little excitement and demonstration as possible. Hence you do not know perhaps who I am, nor does it matter. I want you to know however, and you will in time find out, that I have been sent here by those who are your true friends. And that the producers and laboring men of this country can depend upon them, and upon me in your time of need. as being true to your interests and faithful in your service. Our mission is, to endeavor to institute means to better your condition. But this explanation may not fully satisfy you. Like your chairman, many of you doubtless, are anxious to know what my politics are. And I will try to tell you briefly: I am an American citizen, and a practical believer in the principles upon which this government was founded. I want to pull down, and humble the aristocratic and arrogant millionaires. And elevate and encourage the worthy poor. I want legislation that will restrain the rich in their greed and avarice, and reduce their surplus wealth and income. And that at the same time will reduce the cost of living to those in poor or moderate circumstances, at least one half, and correspondingly increase their earnings.

And I want to take what your politicians call protection, from the opulent aristocrats of the East, and give it to the farmers and laboring men of the West. And I want to select men as law makers, who will go to our State and National capital as men employed and well paid for their services, in any position of trust and responsibility. And who at least will try to render an equivalent for money paid them, and confidence placed in them, by doing something of practical benefit for the people who send them there for that purpose. And not devote their time to the interest of cliques and combinations, who are defrauding those who thus send them. And I want much less red tape buncombe, and more practical common sense and fidelity exercised in the interests of laboring men generally, on the part of those who make and execute the laws. And I will not stop at merely saying I wanted these things: I will have it so, if you will follow my directions, and you are even one-half as true to your obligations as citizens as you ought to be. You have ample power and means to do this, quietly and orderly at the polls. And if you neglect making an effort in self defense much longer I have no promises or pledges to give you. If it is possible that you have become so inexcusably dilatory and unconcerned about your own and families condition and welfare, as to let these scheming and unscrupulous politicians, of either party, lead you around by the nose any longer. Or if it be possible that fate has decreed that you have procrastinated until the doors of liberty and the poor man's rights have been closed and bolted against you, by your enemies, and in your presence, without even raising your hand to prevent it, the future historian will hold you justly responsible for the failure of the best and most liberal government, God ever gave to man. And the cringing and servile votaries of pompous aristocracy, whose groveling nature begets the belief that a citizens claim to respect is measured by their income and money, no matter how obtained, would complacently tally one more victory for perpetuating the rich man's arrogance, opulence and oppression, and the poor man's humility, poverty and submission. And if there is any words in our language, the meaning of which, the rising generation should be taught to despise, it is these. Those are some of my sentiments, or politics if you prefer that term. And your chairman here, or any others, need no longer remain in doubt as to where I stand thus far. His audience by this time is no longer able to restrain their feelings, and applause in the usual way not being sufficient to satisfy them, three cheers for the stranger, is proposed. And the speaker, seeing their enthusiasm was beyond control, became resigned and said: O well, go on and relieve yourselves. And they were given with a hearty goodwill. But, continued the old patriot, I have heard of your cheering political buncombe. so much that you need not expect that I will regard it as much of a compliment until you act as well as cheer. What I want you to do is to calmly consider these things, and then if they accord with your views I want you to act promptly, and in a determined manner, and never let up or waver in sentiment or action until you obtain these results. Then you can cheer, and have cause to be happy. And God grant I may be enabled to help you cheer and celebrate such a victory. But applauding political stump orators for telling you stories, prepared solely for the purpose of getting your votes, to enable them to defraud you, or at mere mention of true reform, and doing nothing in a practical way to obtain it, ought to be shamefully unworthy of your credence or toleration.

I find you are divided in political sentiment and action. Some of you voting for and working with what you call Republicans. And others as zealously supporting Democrats, Prohibitionists &c. Well you have been trying this for a long time, and it seems to me that the experience you have had, and are now having, ought to satisfy you farmers and laboring men if anything will. A person may be deceived and swindled once by one they had reason to believe was a true friend, and not have their judgment called in question much for this one mistake. But if they continued to let the same rascal deceive and defraud them time after time, you would all say they needed a guardian. You certainly must know, if you but observe and think, that a contest be-

tween these politicians, has come to be one simply for honors and
spoils, and one in which very little attention is paid to ther rights or
interests of the masses, except when they do so far the purpose of
getting your votes to obtain the position sought.· You certainly must
have observed that the stronger either party becomes, and the longer
they remain in power the more corrupt they become. And if you men
who work at manual labor for a living, are foolish enough to stick to
them any longer, the wisest thing you can do, is to vote with the weak-
est, for the nearer equal they are. the more honest they are compelled
to be.

But has it ever occurred to you. that when you show your party zeal,
and argue and quarrel over the issues party leaders set up, generally
for the purpose of catching your votes, that you are doing the very
thing that pliable politicians, and lords of capital generally, want you to
do. They well know that the masses, or workingmen of this nation,
have the power in their own hands, if you but sensibly determined to
utilize it for your own benefit and protection, and as we of revolutionary
times intended it should be used. They well know that if you would
sensibly conclude to throw your political and party affiliations and preju-
dices to the dogs, and unite for your own interest and protection, and all
laboring men, and those in sympathy with them, all vote and pull together for their constitutional rights, or if even one half of them would
do so, that they, the capitalists &c., would gradually. and some of them
suddenly, have to get down where they legitimately belong. And that
the milli ons of your money, unjustly legislated into the vaults of mo
nopolies and millionaires, and often supporting all kinds of pomp, extravagance and vice, might possibly have to be returned in some legal
way to the rightful owners, and put to much better use in supporting
commendable industry, and providing more comfortable homes and
better surroundings for the worthy poor. And please understand, that
I want nothing I have said or may say, construed to mean that I am op-
posed to persons accumulating a liberal competence, or even becoming
wealthy, if done in a fair and legitimate way. The right of people in
this country to the benefit of their industry, energy, genius or frugality,
must be as free and unrestrained, as their right to life, liberty and the
pursuit of happiness. And I will go further, and say that if wealth
and influence is obtained by the fair and legitimaie use of any one, or all
of these faculties, it is even so far, commendable and praise worthy.
But mark you, if these restrictions even, had been enforced or respected, the word millionaire would not be needed in your dictionary.
And when we come to consider the question of equal rights, our field of
vision widens, and we begin to wonder whether or not this gentleman

who has grown so vastly rich, has made it all in this way, without infringing the rights of other citizens, who are more dependent. Or has
he obtained it by scheming and plotting, in utter disregard of others
rights in moderate or poor circumstances. Or still worse has he combined with other rich and unscrupulous schemers for this purpose, and
for setting traps to catch and defraud the unsuspecting public. And if
so, it is a very different thing, and becomes a dangerous public evil that
must not be tolerated in this country. It must always be remembered
that as wealth and influence increases, that the obligations and responsi-
bilities of good citizenship, which includes a decent regard for others
rights, increases correspondingly and must be held to account. Hence,
when those thus favored become so regardless of these obligations as to
use these potent factors for good and evil, for the purpose of cheating
and defrauding their less fortunate fellow citizens, or in any way to corrupt or influence legislation for selfish ends, or to hinder or influence
the free use of the elective franchise, they become dangerous public
evils, and just legislation must and will restrain or punish such crimes
against public justice. That money and the influence it brings, has
been and is now freely used to influence voting in all your political parties, and even in your halls of legislation, and by the consent and sanction of many you have placed in high positions of trust and power, I
have evidence that fully convinces me. And this is an admission I
will be compelled to make in our report. humiliating as it may be, to
those who sent us.

But these are not the only causes of your political misfortune, and it
is but just to allude to one other, that I regard as the most prolific of evil
results, and that is the slothfulness and consequent ignorance, and lack
of appreciation and respect for our country and its privileges, on the
part of so many of the laboring classes, as you now call them, and especially so in large cities. This thought must seem extremely humiliating to all good citizens, who naturally feel a deep interest in the present
and future welfare of our country, and realize the urgent need of political reform, and know also how indifferent and unreliable many such
unfortunates are. and what a hindrance to just and equitable measures
of any kind obtained by the ballot. For, not having adequate knowledge of rights and privileges, they do not comprehend or appreciate.
And knowing little and caring less how the government is run as long
as they can procure a mere subsistance, they become the willing tools of
scheming and unscrupulous politicians, who knowing that their vote
counts as much as any others, use them to the best advantage, often as
hirelings to offset and even overcome the votes of the better class of
citizens. And for this reason these same politicians are quite generally
becoming more successful office seekers, as you call them, than upright.

honorable men, who will not stoop to such vile practices. In this way the scum of New York City has more than once decided who was to be your President for the next four years.

Much of the cause of such humiliating conditions is attributed to foreigners, prematurely made citizens. But, when the effects of wrongdoing become so apparrant, it is quite natural to try to shift the blame onto other shoulders. But the facts seem to be, that many political office seekers and demagogues whose appreciation and respect for the privileges we secured for citizens were about of a kind the devil would be supposed to have for making an acceptable minister of the Gospel. Designedly misconstrued our intentions in founding this government, into national vanity and political buncombe, to induce foreigners to come here by the ship load, and the more credulous they were, the better for their purpose. And on their arrival crowd them into full fledged citizenship soon as possible. What for? Does any one, native or naturalized, believe that this was prompted by a desire to better the condition of these people? As well might they believe that the manufacturers and venders of patent medicines were instigated in their efforts solely by a desire to preserve your health. It was generally done because this class of politicians wanted more voters, who could be duped by flattery and appeals to their national sympathies, and their votes thus secured to elect many such schemers to high positions they but dishonored and disgraced. But the end and the means to that end, must be both looked after, and foreigners must be required to furnish reasonable evidence of ability and desire to cast an intelligent vote. If they cannot help to cleanse the putrid condition of your body politics, they at least should be restrained from producing any more septic poison in its system. Of course even this reasonable demand, would cause some of your political wolves to howl about such imposition on the suffering Irish, industrious Germans &c. But just let them howl. What we want from this oh, in this line, is foreigners who are thoughtful and considerate enough to appreciate the blessings of a free government and the privileges we give them, and who will realize that such requirements will promote the ultimate good of all citizens alike, whether native or naturalized, and who will be even glad to assist us, as well as themselves, in furnishing all the rights and privileges these schemers talked of so glibly, but only for the purpose of getting votes and aid in their own evil designs. But let me whisper in your ears, that justice may demand that the foreigner question be kept a little quiet for a while, until you straighten things up a little closer home. Those who have glass houses you know, &c.

Since our arrival here in the west, we have found that you have one or more self-constituted political bosses in almost every voting precinct, who arrogantly boast of the influence they can exercise over you farmers and workingmen when you come to vote. These are the fellows, political schemers of larger caliber use as the most efficient tools to accomplish their evil designs here among you, and as inducements of some kind is necessary to stimulate their cheek and industry, the promise of a county office, or perhaps member of assembly is held out for their acceptance, and as things are generally run, I find they are the ones who usually get there. And this is about the way it is done: A schemer in one township, who thinks his time has come to get an office, will visit his co-workers in other townships, who of course want an office too, as soon they can get it. Schemer No. 1, wants them to have their township support him, and promises that when they come out as candidates, he will see that his township goes solid for them. All are agreed, the matter is now in shape, and these fellows look very wise and commence telling you at every opportunity what a nice man the other fellow is, and what a good officer he would make. And when nominated for the position sought, the political papers of the party, in that locality will compliment and congratulate you, who are the victims of this chicanery, for having made so wise a choice in selecting a man so eminently qualified to fill the office in a worthy and creditable manner, and in he goes with a big majority, and you are once more called upon to rejoice over a grand Republican or Democratic victory. For higher offices, including those of your State and for Congress, your political farce is manipulated generally in about the same way, only on a larger scale, and on the principle that the greater the prize and doubt of obtaining it, the greater the scheming and intrigue necessary to secure it. Money is freely used in these contests between your political gladiators, especially when victory is doubtful. And the most able schemers or in other words, the fellow who can do the most attractive talking, tell the most funny stories, and influence the most votes, gets a correspondingly large share for his eminent services, and is generally a rising star for Congress or some other big office, and when they enter the field are lauded as model men by other aspirants in the party, traveling the same road. And the political papers of the party will vie with each other in referring with just pride to his political record and eminent services to the party, and explain in the most affecting and pathetic terms how much you are indebted to him for his past valuable services and untiring zeal in your behalf. Then the circus opens, ringmasters enter, and political buncombe in the way of speeches, rallies and torch light processions follow in regular succession. You then go to the polls, and under the influence of the excitement thus produced, cast a vote that but encourages a continuance of such practices. This can be accounted for only on the ground that these political contests are purposely got up to excite the masses; knowing as they do that as excitement increases, sense or judgement correspondingly weakens. But it occurs to me that after such excitement blows over, and you voters cool down to sober thought, and look around and consider your surroundings and condition in life as compared with these same politicians and others, and then come to pay the interest on your mortgaged homes, with little prospect of ever owning them again, and then an exorbitant tax on the equity you still own, and on the other fellows share too, and then another high tax on nearly everything you eat, wear or use, that some of your political benefactors call protection, and then estimate the general market value of your hard labor and its products, and the actual cost of supporting yourselves and families even in the most plain and frugal manner, and then add as an appendage to your calculations, the fact that you are the victims of fraudulent monopolies, rings, trusts &c., got up by avaricious, scheming capitalists, many of whom are piling up wealth until it becomes millions, and so easy that it hardly requires an effort on their part after their scheme is concocted, and all this under legal sanction. It occurs to me I repeat, that you would have evidence enough to convince you, if any thing will, how much you are indebted to most of these politicians you have been electing to make your laws and protect your interests, for their untiring efforts and zeal in your behalf. Yes, I should think you would. For my part, when I think of the efforts and pluck it required to make this a government of and for the people, and then after the lapse of a century, come back here and find that you have voluntarily surrendered most of the rights and privileges transmitted to you for your safe keeping, and submit to be thus duped and imposed upon by these smooth and arch deceivers, I feel like shaking you up. If your wives and school children could have a clear conception of how you have been bamboozled by some of these political sharks, I can't see how they could, with confidence, look up to you as husbands, parents or protectors, until you resolve to abandon your party buncombe and assert your rights as citizens, and demand faithful service from your legislators and others placed in power by your votes.

I have been among your national dignitaries before I came here, and observed them closely, and am fully convinced that if you expect any relief or good, for you, to come out of politics, until you wake up to the necessity of re-constructing your political fabric in selecting men to serve you, you are doomed to disappointment, just as much as you would be if you were expecting the vile weeds to cease growing in your corn fields without any effort to exterminate them. Your U. S. senators are, so far as I could see, with few exceptions, a batch of pompous, aristocratic millionaires, whose manners, actions, customs and inclinations are as foreign to your needs as are the lords of England. Your congressmen are mostly bankers, lawyers and politicians, whose time is mostly occupied in attending fashionable resorts, preparing buncombe speeches and assisting other members from distant localities in procuring appropriations for government contracts. Some I seen there, were I believe well disposed and conscientious, but many of them were a kind of genteel, modest do-nothings, who incline to venerate wealth and display. They seemed too nice or too timid or something to even offer an objection when fraudulent combinations were pitted against the people's rights. And if you had no other choice, you had much better elect an aggressive man, even though comparatively illiterate, with barely intelligence enough to know and plucky enough to express, like Davy Crocket did, that he could not talk as well as they could, but he could lick any man in the house, and then proceed to do so, if he could do nothing more commendable than to send one of your slick, genteel, fastidious, well meaning do-nothings, who sit there like a bound boy at a husking, afraid or too nice or worthless or something to even interpose an objection, when millions of your money, the product of this fertile soil and your hard labor, is being appropriated and squandered to build coast and harbor defences, rifled canon, iron clad gun-boats and costly and ornamental public buildings generally let at two or three times the actual cost of the work to be done, and often altogether unnecessary, except to afford political pets a chance for profitable investment.

But you have other choices, plenty of them, men who if you will hunt them up and send them there as your legal representatives, you will soon hear of a racket in Congress. Men who realize that this is the people's government, and poor man's as well as the rich man's, and that the national capital with all its spacious apartments, adornment and contents is yours as well as theirs, and that there is a great many more of you than there is of them, and that every legal voter is an equal partner in the whole concern, and hence men who will feel perfectly at home, and have the common sense and self respect to regard the biggest toad in the puddle as a social and political equal, but never a superior, unless that distinction is due for having been more upright and useful to their fellow men, and that would let most of those fellows out. Men who will tell them forcibly, firmly and respectfully that they have been making laws that make the rich richer and the poor poorer, and that they have been sent to try and reverse this process in a quiet way, to see how it will work, and that the farmers and laboring men of their districts have been liberally furnished by their honorable body, with high taxes, starvation prices for their products, and hard times, all the appropriations and profits going to the monopolies and rich capitalists directly or indirectly, and that even a temporary reversal of this program would be a relief to the over taxed brains and flabby muscles of the dainty millionaires, and dudes who admire them, and at least equally advantagious to the overtaxed muscles and empty purses of the toiling masses. How can we get such men, do you ask. You have plenty of such, but they must be sought after. They will not, as a rule, get down to ask an office, nor solicit your support in the murky pool, politics has got to be. But O, my friends, when I think of how long you have utterly neglected your plain duty to yourselves, your family and your country, and how often you have been deceived by schemers on one side calling themselves good Republicans, and on the other side, good Democrats &c. And how willingly you walk right into the traps they set for you. called platforms and issues, and which they seldom have any use for after election. My hope for the future of our country is almost turned into despair. When I remember how well it was understood that the people would be the rightful rulers, and legalowners of this country, and those whom they selected to make, interpret or execute their laws would be their public servants. What, I ask, do we understand this to mean. I understand that a servant is one subject to, or under the control of another to a reasonable extent, and so far only as relates to the particular service to be performed for a stipulated consideration, and in this limited sense, the party for whom the service is performed may be considered a master, and in this sense one of your most worthy presidents and a martyr to the cause of liberty, adopted this principle as a rule of action, that public officials were public servants, and the people who elected them were their rightful masters.

Now think of this for a moment. Are we to consider this free government a mere farce? No, no, from several voices. Well then, are we to conclude that these principles and conditions of citizenship are but silly, impracticable jargon. Why if we put this in the way I now find prevalent, how will we have it? Why, almost if not altogether the directly opposite conditions. The ones whose rights is to be masters in this matter, has become subject too, and controled by the ones whose province is to be servants. After you elect your so-called public servants now, they soon become your public masters, and some of them arrogant and tyranical ones at that, who instead of looking up to you as masters or even as constituents, look down upon you from their lofty perch, as unworthy of consideration or even notice. Why a short time ago my companions and I were the guests of your senators and congressmen in your country's capital, and the pomp, grandeur and extravagance of themselves, their homes and amusements made us tired of their opulent ease and luxury. And one evening while they were favoring us, as they seemed to think, with what they called a grand banquet, my friend, Observer here, quietly walked up to where we were sitting and in a becoming and sensible way, asked for my attention, and as he done so, the assembled aristocrats and fashionable dudes of that assembly, seemed horrified at his appearance in plain garb, and gazed at him with a shudder of surprise and disgust, as though he was a cannibal from the Fiji Islands. But to us it was a great relief to meet even one man in that gorgeous assembly who looked like a sensible and natural American. (Here the pent up feelings of his audience again burst forth in applause,) and the old patriot continued: On our arrival here among you farmers and laboring men, we found a slight change in conditions and actions. O yes, the contrast was so great I have not the command of language to do either justice, but after my first observations and talk with my friends, John and Mary here, if I had been required by those who sent me, to briefly describe in writing, the shape I found these masters and servants, we have been talking about, in, I should have put it something like this: I found the servants, their families and attendants, living in splendid mansions, provided and adorned in gorgeous magnificance, reveling in opulent ease and luxury. I found the masters in cheap and ragged clothes, with rough and bleeding hands, out in the cold November winds from daylight until dark, toiling over the rough and frozen ground, husking 16 cent corn, and their wives and children toiling in a way no less laborous and fatigueing. Their general condition, considered in connection with their mortgaged homes, and many without any homes, oppressive taxes and general prospects under the way political matters are now conducted, seems to me discouraging and heart rending—a pause—and he continues in subdued tones: O, for shame, my indifferent, unappreciative and ungrateful fellow countrymen, must it be said that you have proved thus recreant to the most exalted and liberal trust ever committed to man's keeping. Is it true, can it be true that the most generous and liberal sentiments that ever originated in the brain of the patriots and philanthropists of seventy-six, and defended by them against the armies of a powerful and unscrupulous tyrant for six long years of hardship, suffering and danger, will thus finally result in building up and maintaining a hateful and abominable set of arrogant aristocrats, such as we then and there, labored so long and so faithfully to pull down. In those memorable struggles, many of us were compelled to walk barefooted over the rough and frozen ground, we suffered untold hardships at Stillwater, Brandywine and Valley Forge. In the time of our greatest distress and privation, affluence and ease was offered us. to become the subjects of tyrants. No we replied, we are poor and destitute, but poor as we are, the king of England is not rich enough to buy us.

And now, old and feeble as I am, I would without a murmur, concent to undergo the same hardships and danger for a like period, rather than surrender one jot of the principals then defended. I could not endure it now, I would fall by the wayside, but I would hold out as long as God gave me life and strength to move, rather than see these poor children of yours when they grow up to be men and women, subject to such cruel and heartless oppression, as we were before we united in self-defence. (Here again his audience lost control of their feelings. Sobs were heard from all parts of the house,) and the old patriot waited and reflected, he turned to speak to the chairman and found him in tears. He then looked at observer and found him too deeply affected for utterance. A stranger in the audience now arose and asked to be permitted to say a few words, which being freely granted, he said: The speaker was an entire stranger to him, but who ever you are or what ever you · are or wherever you come from, God bless you, for what you have said this evening. Would to God it would continue to sound in the ears of every mechanic, farmer and laboring man in this broad land, until they resolve to unite in self-defence and carry it into effect. (Applause.) I have thought much about these things, and it seems we are sinking lower and lower, and that if something is not done we will soon have no right to defend that is worthy of the name, and fear that resort to the bullet will be the ultimate result. He resumed his seat and the old patriot continues, I thank you my friend for your appreciation and heartily agree with you as to the neccessity of uniting in self-defence of your rights. But we want no bullets or people who will resort to such means in this country. Where recourse is had to the ballot, there is no earthly excuse for the bullet, but ignorance and moral cowardice, while exceptional cases there may be where it had to be used in defence of right and justice with good results. No such claim is possible now. In a government like this the sympathy of all good and intelligent people is on your side and such constitute a host of your effective strength; that you dare not to tamper with, and to retain their sympathy and respect you must keep within proper bounds and work in a quiet and orderly way. Intelligently used the ballot will bring you sure victory and with it respect and prosperity. The bullet will bring you nothing but defeat and humiliation.

Public matters cannot long remain entire secrets, politicians you elect and confide in may play the knave secretly and betray your confidence in the interest of your enemies, and do so a way that although quite generally believed, cannot be proven, but it is only a question of time if there is much of such rascality, it will prove itself. Results will tell the tale. They are telling on the masses of this country now and have been for some time in a way that leaves no room for doubt, and, as a result and proof of the magnitude of their crimes, you have millionaires by the thousands, and as a natural consequence about one hundred times as many poor. You have opulent, arrogant, aristocrats and humble slaves to toil and drudgery, and this in a country where it is a free-for-all race. and every man is supposed to be his own master.

Why some of your rich nabobs whose hearts have not yet became calloused to every feeling of humanity and every principle of justice, I found at times were ashamed of their vast wealth and its rapid increase. Often without an effort on their part while the fact was staring them in the face that thousands of their fellow citizens, who are equally as sensative and more worthy, are toiling and struggling against fate, misfortune and poverty to obtain a mere subsistance for themselves and families. This is also known and will have its effect if but agitated and the people wake up from their lethargy.

But the crises is almost here. There is a time when patience and forberance ceases to be virtues. If you persist in showing no disposition to help yourselves in an effective way you will be considered unworthy of the assistance of others, who will then be compelled to adopt the selfish conclusion that they will look out for themselves, and if you rashly resort to force of numbers, and arbitray and coercive measures or mob-law. defeat and more stringent laws will be the result.

Strikes of laboring men, mechanics and artizens for an increase in wages and reduction of the hours of labor, I find is becoming a matter of every day occurance. The rapid accumulation and concentration of the wealth alluded to, has expanded many corporations into such vast and varied proportion that the force of such men often required in one such concern, numbers thousands. And when wares or needed articles of any kind are manufactured for public use and sold to dealers, or when public convenience is dependent upon the products of their labor or skill, so many such men abandoning their posts, without giving due notice of their intentions are guilty of great wrong. Inasmuch as they inflict inconvenience and loss upon an unoffending public, who are in no way to blame for the grievences complained of, and this works adversely for them. On public sentiment and sympathy, and so far the vily capitalist is safe. He knows the value of these mighty factors, but when such men determine to enforce redress. and not only abandon their work, but also organize to prevent others who may be willing to do the same work for the pay they refused, they are guilty of an act that all good citizens will regard as the laboring man's greatest misfortune, and which all intelligent people, all over this land, whose hearts, sentiments and sympathies are in full accord with laboring men and their interests, and who are but waiting for an opportunity to do all they can in a quiet and legitimate way for the cause of labor, as against capital, will regard it as dark clouds of mere physical force and blunders, obscuring the sunshine of liberty and equal rights.

Such movements may be of some use, as evidence of the dissatisfaction of these men under existing conditions, and hence the necessity of investigating the cause and applying a remedy. But as a means of securing more favorable recognition of their rights or more liberal pay for their services. They are serious and mischievous blunders, for if concessions are made at times to their demands, it will only be temporary, and because the wily capitalist is afraid of their combined strength, but they furnish this same capitalist just the pretense he desires to secure, an increase in the military force of the country, and that is just what they will do through their willing co-workers in halls of legislation. If these strikes continue, until in addition to their backing millions of money, they will also be backed by a sufficient force of canon and bayonets, to be masters of the situation, strike or no strike. Of course these soldiers, called National Guards, will be organized ostensibly to repell invasion and suppress riot, and it is but fair to admit that the frequency and magnitude of these strikes may reasonably be regarded as a menace or indication of such a disturbance. Of course those who lead or engage in them may think differently and claim that as long as they are conducted in an orderly way, that they have at least as much right to combine for protection as the corporations have to keep grinding them down, and it would seem so, but the facts are, both go beyond the limit of fair and legitimate rights in doing so. On the capitalist side it is an unwarrantable abuse of power that should not be tolerated in a country like this, and in the strikers case it is the wrong way to combine for redress. The wily capitalist has adroitly succeeded in getting nearly all the legislation in his favor, and there is always danger of his shrewd and unscrupulous encroachments on labor, being gradually submitted totoo long, but not so in the striker case. Such acts by large bodies of such men, however orderly, will always be regarded by peaceable and well disposed citizens with suspicion of approaching disturbance and danger, just as we regard a dark and threatning cloud with apprehensions of an approaching storm, although it may never come. It must be admitted that in thus trying to protect what they regard as their rights, they are infringing on the rights of other citizens. When an innocent public suffer inconven-

iences or loss as a result of such strikes, and besides this others whose
rights must be equally respected or often debarred the free exercise
thereof by fear of danger, if nothing more of taking places abandoned by
the strikers, however much they may desire the employment.   The facts
are, capital has always lorded it over labor, and always will until labor
substitutes intelligent action for physical force.

Do not understand me to mean that farmers, mechanics and laboring men should not combine for self protection. It is the very thing I
want you to do, but not in turbulent demonstrations and strikes, but at
the ballot box, and not a farmers union here, a mechanics union there,
and a knights of labor union somewhere else, and like a balky team,
no two pulling together. But a grand union of all these interests combined, so far as possible, all over the land, organized to go in a quiet
and orderly way to the polls, and thus gain a victory worthy of American freemen, and one that will make the millionaire and monopolist
tremble in their boots at the just retribution approaching, and restore
just rights, and honorable and effective means os self protection and support to thousands of downcast and deserving poor, who have labored and
toiled and struggled against oppression, misfortune and penury all their
lives, and nothing to show for it but the extravagant and pompous display of the favored ones, into whose vaults their hard earnings has been
continually drifting, as a result of class and unscrupulous legislation.

And even this kind of combination might be regarded as unnecessary
and objectionable in a country like ours. But plotting capitalists and
their co-workers, in office, have combined to rake in your hard earned
money, and influence legislation to dignify extortion and fraud with
legal sanction.   Under just laws the farmers and laboring men of this
country would need no such combination or protection, more than such
laws, and their faithful execution, would give them.   But as it is, combined effort is your only hope.

Your Farmer's Alliance is in most respects commendable and ben-
eficial in a social, moral and educational sense.   The occupation of
farming naturall tends to isolation, and such an organization will
bring you into closer communion and fellowship, beget more desire for
reading and investigation, and widens your field of observation.

But as an effective and adequate remedy for the great primary and
national evil of political corruption, which is the fountain head from
whence all the lesser evils flow, that you have any cause to complain of,
and in this way trying to combat it, is like taking the little pills of the
Homeopathist to cure a long standing and malignant disease, or skirm-
ishing around in squads to capture a well fortified position, that will require the united effort of all your combined forces.   This is the source

against which you must combine to repel invasion, but I fear it is not
the kind your soldiers are intended for.

Your combining to procure the goods you need, from parties at a dis-
tance, because you can in this way get them cheaper than your home
dealers sell such, is perfectly justifiable if your home dealers enter a
combination to compel you to pay their prices. But as long as they rely
upon their own merits and efforts, and keep out of these trusts or combinations of any kind, and willing to meet fair competition, it is on
your part, penny-wise and pound-foolish. When each dealer acts for
himself, and it is a free-for-all race, the law of supply and demand
and competition in trade will be all the protection you need or can
reasonably expect in this line. Your interests, and those of your home
merchants are identical, and they cannot afford, even if so disposed.
which is always doubtful until proved, to be otherwise than fair and
reasonable in their methods and prices. And hence I believe it is folly,
except for the reasons mentioned. In fact it looks to me, something
like being tickled with a straw, and striking a blow at an imaginary
bug hard enough to hurt yourselves, and paying no attention to the political gallinippers, that are sucking at your life blood.

But I suppose your case is something like the people of a village or
neighborhood, who had been impoverished by theft long continued, but
who were unable to find the guilty ones. In such case, the first unfortunate stragler detected with nimble fingers, would at once be suspicioned of all the stealing that had been done, or at least accessory to it.
So in your case perhaps to some extent. You have been deceived and
cheated so long by politicians and their favored pets, that its effects
are becoming self evident, and you cannot but know that there is a big
leak somewhere, and not clearly understanding the real cause, you
naturally become suspicious of the motives, of those, with whom you
transact business. And when you find one of your merchants has
sold you an article for even a trifle more than you could have got the
same for elsewhere, or beat you in a little trade when perhaps you were
just as anxious to get the best of it as they were, you are apt to conclude that all the business men you deal with are trying to beat you.
and that this is the chief cause of your stringent circumstances.

This is but an evidence of weakness. Such petty grievances will
naturally occur as long as people are differently constituted, and must
be included in the ups and downs of life, in which you must look out for
yourselves.

Political maladministration and general unfaithfulness on the part of
those politicians, who promise you relief solely for the purpose of getting
your support, and the condition of affairs such a course will naturally

engender, is all you can have any just cause to complain of in this
country. And however bad this may be, it is to a very considerable
extent the legitimate result of your own apathy, indifference and negligence, and hence it would be more creditable to abandon, so far as you
can, this ineffectual and humiliating way of seeking redress. Complaining, as a rule, is an evidence of weakness, fault finding is no vir-
tue, nobody likes a growler, and patience and forbearance much longer,
on the part of farmers and laboring men, in this case would be but another name for incompetency and moral cowardice. What I have said
here to-night, I have done for the purpose of trying to wake you up
to a sense of your condition and danger. You have the power in your
own hands, but to be masters of the situation and merit the respect or
even sympathy of your fellow men, you must show to the world that you
know this and know also how to use this power when necessary for your
own protection. You will not, you cannot my friends, merit the decent
regard of thinking intelligent people here or elsewhere much longer unless you at least make a faithful effort to do this. The humility and
poverty of the masses in most of Europe, who are the unfortunate subjects of tyrants with unlimited power, appeals to our own sympathy and
we think how intelligent and happy many of such poor creatures might
be if they only had a fair chance. But, in a country like this where
natural and conventional advantages are second to none on the globe,
where every inducement possible is held out to every one to make the
most of life in a legitimate and honorable way. Poverty or menial conditions is regarded in an altogether different light, and unless the results
of bodily condition, or destructive and uncontrollable agencies, I look
upon with a strong suspicion of something very discreditable back of it,
and rightfully so. So I repeat I do not complain too much of your de-
privation or poverty. We secured for you the right to be free and inde-
pendent citizens; we put the power to rule in the hands of the working
men to run this government or have it run in their interest, and that is
all we could do. All you have to do is to use that power with discretion
and some sense to make your homes happy and prosperous. If you are
not willing to make even a reasonable effort to that end, and if your producers and laboring men will not do that much for your own welfare and
that of your children, and protection from tyranical inroads of greedy
capital, what more (in the name of Heaven,) I ask, can or could we do?
We could not institute a government in which people would prosper
without an effort, or where careless, indolent sluggards, or even those
who are lacking in the necessary ability would be as desirably provided
for as intelligent, industrious persons, with good business qualifications.
And who would want such a condition of affairs, even if it was possible.

All any government can do, is to encourage commendable effort, and this ours has done in the most liberal manner possible. But it seems all do not improve the opportunity, and of course none will profit by such concessions but those who do. And it would therefore be unfair and unjust to regard wealth, within reasonable bounds, as any evidence of knavery, or poverty as of itself any evidence of honesty. Men with necessary qualifications and strong desire to accumulate, will always come out ahead iu the race for wealth, if they do not for happiness. And lazy, indolent loafers will as surely come out behind. One naturally drifts toward business success, the other as naturally toward poverty. One thinks the world, and especially America, is good enough for him. and rolls up his sleeves, if necessary, and goes to work with a will, and determination to succeed. All he asks is a fair chance and equal rights, and that he will have. The other turns his attention to brooding over his misfortunes, and doesn't regard them exactly as blessings in disguise, but inclines to find fault with every thing in general and persons who are prospering iu particular, as if they wished everybody to think the country would be better off without them. These are matters of individual traits and concern, that legislation was not intended to reach, and I mention it because these are some of the arguments you will have to meet. It is the province of law in this country to protect each citizen, and especially the weaker, in the free exercise of these rights, or in other words, the most protection for those citizens who need the most. Hence, when two or more of these wise. ambitious fellows, allow their desire for wealth to beget a total disregard for other's rights, who need and deserve government protection more than they, because weaker in this sense, and they go beyond the bounds of legitimate business, and organize rings, trusts and other fraudulent combinations to compel the unprotected citizen in poor or moderate circumstances to pay their price for what the mass of the people have to buy, and accept their price for what you people have to sell. and these prices so established as to constitute a system of public robbery, and even influence legislation and obtain legal aid. In such nefarious practices they become a virulent poison to the life blood of American liberty, and must be promptly suppressed, or this free country becomes a mockery and a by-word. If the kind of government you have now, does not protect industrious and well disposed citizens, because they are in poor or only moderate circumstances. from such rascally encroachments of capital in the hands of unscrupulous sharks, I ask, what is it good for? Is it worth to you farmers and laborers, the tax you are required to pay each year for its support? Has it become destructive of the ends it was established to protect and foster, and if it

has, what is the right of the people in such a case, who do you understand the word people to mean in this country, and what are you here
for? Give this matter a moment's sober thought, and then see if you
will not agree with me when I say that it is a duty more imperative
upon the massess of this country than any other I know of at this time,
to God or man, to combine regardless of party, and by your votes stamp
out such nefarious frauds, and at once change such political practices
on your part, as have proved instrumenral in leading to such corruption
and turn over a new leaf, and for Heaven's sake and for humanity's
sake drop, for the present at least, all your squabbling on such questions
as temperance, prohibition, high or low license, tariff and free trade and
even on religion, which although all worthy of attention more or less are
yet, at least in a temporal sense, of but trifling moment when compared
with the grand doctrine of equal rights, equal justice and equal privileges to all citizens, rich or poor, and protection for the weaker, and
unite to secure faithful representation and laws to maintain these ends,
which in a great measure will also settle many of your minor differences
And now I will give you an opportunity to consider this matter, and
may I hope that you will decide to act promptly and faithfully Yes, yes,
from all parts of the house. Well then to-morrow morning at 9 o'clock I
will meet a few of the older and more experienced men for consultation
as how to proceed with the work at this place. Good-night.

The feelings of his audience were much too deeply affected by this
time to indulge in noisy applause and all retired quietly and thought-
fully, impressed with convictions that they were there to stay, but wheth
er or not all of those thus impressed would prove to have the courage of
these convictions is yet to be tried.

The old patriot expected but a chosen few at his consultation meeting
next morning, but it became evident at an early hour that the enthusiasm caused by his talk was going to be wide spread and general. He
noticed this and seemed to regard it unfavorably. It seems, he said to
Observer, that the effect of your visit and talk on these people is chiefly
emotional and I fear they will be too fickle and irresolute to overcome
the difficulties that will be thrown in their way by wily politicians and
their coworkersi in the public press. Well, replied Observer, I hope and
believe you will be agreeably dissapointed in this case. Well if I am it
will be more than agreeable replied the old patriot, it will make me shout
for joy and I will be hopeful and patient as I can. Just then a number
of vehicles came along filled with occupants on their way to the meeting
and when the old man was observed, cheer after cheer from the men
and many a God bless you from the women went up for their old friend.
The hour for meeting was now at hand, and they start for the school

house, and as they approach it soon becomes evident that the house would not contain one-fourth of the people assembled. And it being a beautiful autumn morning, a stand has been erected outside for the speaker, tastefully ornamented, and a deputation of ladies dressed in appropriate colors, had been selected to conduct the old man to his seat. Observer expected all this, but feared that his friend's acknowledgment of such honors would hardly be of a kind that would lead them to conclude that such efforts were appreciated. He was pleased however to see that his old friend submitted to the honors with becoming modesty, and as the ladies lead him forward, "Our Country" was sung with a spirit and pathos that evidently surprised and deeply affected him. But yet, when seated on the stand and all eyes upon him, seemed perfectly calm and self possessed. And Observer knowing what was customary to expect from a speaker after such honors shown them, no one in that vast audience was more anxious to hear what the peculiarities of his old friend would suggest, than he. The chairman of the meeting was now observed speaking in a whisper to his friend, which was answered by a significant shake of the head, after which it was announced that the speaker desired no introduction or formality of any kind. This brought smiles to the faces of those who began to know the man, and after a pause the old veteran of '76 arose and said in a strong and firm voice.

My friends, your ideas and customs, and my ideas and way of doing things are evidently quite different, and considering the advantages you enjoy in some respects, and the times you live in, and those in which I lived, and their stern realities, hardships and privations, this I suppose is to be expected, and if I seem to manifest any disregard for any of your ways or customs, it is not from any lack of respect or esteem for you, but because I cannot conform to some of your fashionable ways without acting unnatural, and I prefer to remain true to my own customs and way of doing things, and give you the same privilege.

Were I one of your modern politicians, I suppose I would consider all this enthusiasm and honors shown me by your ladies here, as the most flattering evidence of popularity, and graciously bow my acknowledgments in the most approved style of the art, (laughter) but I am not and never was such as many of them seem to be now. I have come to you as an Aerican citizen to his fellow country-men, and as a father, friend and adviser. For myself individually I have nothing to gain and nothing to lose. But the welfare of our country, and of the toiling masses, who constitute a large majority of its citizens, is everything in this life to me and those who sent me. And the enormous wealth I find among the few, and the general indications of poverty among the many, will, when I report the facts, make the present abode of your

best friends a house of mourning. But it is justly due you to say, that
the evidence you have already furnished me of your willingness to make
an effort in defense of justice and your own rights, will tend to mitigate
their sorrow, and for which you have my sincere thanks, and I trust in
God this feeling will continue to grow stronger until victory for right
and justice will crown your efforts, which it assuredly will if you are but
faithful to your own interests. Our power to help you is of course limited. After securing you the right to decide for yourselves, we cannot
stay here with you, and go to the polls every time you vote, and perhaps
you would not relish such close surveillance. We have given you ample
means of redress in case your rights are infringed. We found they had
been, and after despairing of your making an effective effort in self defence, have come to warn you of approaching danger, and to admonish,
and advise, and beg of you to use these means diligently and sensibly
for your own and our country's protection. Do this, and you will make
us thankful and happy, even if the bouquets and decorations have to be
neglected, and for that matter the enthusiasm and excitement too.
These candid declarations produced a feeling to deep for applause.
Confidence was conspicuous in every face, and Observer was joyful at
the pleasant way his old friend regained his own ground. Some of you
remember, continued the old patriot, that I told you last evening what
the result of these strikes would finally be. This morning the ominous
ring of the deadly winchester rifle in the hands of capitals hirelings in
the streets of Albany is wafted to my ears. Of course the strikers can
arm too, but it would only prove a sad misfortune, that all good citizens
would regret and be compelled to condemn. Did you ever read or hear
of government bayonets or canon being on the side of labor when such
rash and foolish means are resorted too for redress of grievances, real or
imaginary? No, no, the wily capitalists are generally on the safe side
in such strifes. Every intelligent man knows, and every fair minded
man will admit that in the absence of any agreement to the contrary, the
employer has an unquestionable right to discharge his employe at any
time, and that the employe under same conditions has an equal right to
quit his employer's service whenever he wishes. If the employe has acquired a knowledge and adaptability for the vocation he abandoned, for
the purpose of compelling his employer to comply with his demand, and
feels that from long application to its duties and his own negligence to
prevent such a result, that he is disqualified to make any other legitimate
vocation a success, that is no fault of his employer, but the natural result of his own carless habits and willingness to be moulded by such
habits into a helpless and dependant machine, instead of being a free and
independant man and the one who institutes an effective effort to pre-

vent such humilating results, will be entitled to rank as a public benefactor, however much the leaders in the strikes may deserve credit for
their sagacity and good intentions. Able bodied persons reduced to a
condition of poverty or dependance, except as a result of destructive ele-
ments or from some temporary affliction, cannot reasonably expect much
sympathy in a country like this. The humiliation attendant upon failure and the credit accorded success in life is, as a rule, commensurate
with the opportunities afforded to succeed. If you meet a man in the
highway looking uncouth, ignorant, shabby and poor, your natural aversion mellows into sympathy, when you find he has just arrived from a
country in which the poor had no rights, their tyranical rulers were
bound or disposed to respect or notice, and you would feel like saying—
you poor unfortunate wanderer if there is a spark of manhood left in
you after the humiliating conditions you have been subjected to all your
life. you may yet be of some use in a country like this. But if you found
that he had been here many years and although able bodied and of sound
mind, had failed to profit by the opportunities afforded here, your sympathy would now harden into aversion and lack of faith in his ultimate
redemption from penury, now let me say, I did not come here this
morning expecting to talk to a large audience and have only concluded
to say what I have, so as to not entirely dissappoint you. My time is
limited here and I am liable to be called away at any time and I want
to work while here in the way that will do you the most good, and that
will be in attending to the business for which this meeting was intended
Some of the more experienced men here last evening and I will occupy
the room for that purpose, and those of you who remain here can enjoy
yourselves in any way agreeable, and I am sure you will be considerate
and not disturb us with any unnecessary noise. My friend, Observer,
has prepaired and put in place a fac-simile of our old Independance bell,
and if we on the inside agree as to what is needed and how to proceed to
obtain it, the bell will be rung as a signal, then you will have reasons to
at least feel happy in anticipation, but let it be so far as possible a quiet
and hopeful happiness, then waiving a good-bye, the old man started for
the building, followed by the silent admiration and blessings of all.
When he entered the room he found it full of just such men as he wanted, who had purposely occupied it to keep the merely curious from doing
so. Silence and order prevailed as the old man entered and after a moments pause, he requested the doors securely fastened, which being
promptly attended to, he looked over the room, at his new associates with
a strange and effecting expression, in which the different emotions of
sorrow and hope were peculiarly blended.

For the first time since his arrival the tears, which he evidently tried

to conceal, glistened plentifully in the old veterans eyes, and he stood
for a moment in deep reflection.   Finally breaking the silence in a calm
and guarded tone, he said: My friends, It is hardly expected that you
could be affected as I am, it is very seldom that I can be effected to tears
but I confess my feelings were to much for me this time.   After looking
at that bell and the arrangements made to ring it as of old, and then
come to look at the expression on your faces, past scenes and recollec-
tions crowd upon my mind.   A little over one hundred and fourteen
years ago, a smaller number of us than there is here this morning, met
for a purpose that was much more difficult and dangerous to undertake.
The issues to be met then was liberty or bondage, death or victory, but
then and there with tears of retribution for wrongs perpetrated upon us,
we pledged our homes, our honor and our lives, to stand by and defend
to the last, the principles there laid down.   How that promise was kept
you know as well as I do, and that the blessings of liberty and equal
rights were secured for ourselves, our children and posterity.   But none
of us thought then, nor can it be reasonably expected now, that the
rights and privileges the re secured for citizens of our country are self-re-
pairing or self-protecting.   Like all other good and desirable things or
conditions, they well deserve and must have the care and attention of
those who receive their benefit.   But it is unnecessary to repeat the use
you made of such privileges.   Almost criminal neglect on one hand and
a willingness on the other to take advantage of such neglect to the fullest
extent to enrich themselves at your expense and effectually influencing
many of your legislators to render them aid in thus robbing you, briefly
describes the situation.   This was at first done cautiously and in a small
way, but finding that you would gradually yield to such impositation
they are getting so, their rascally scheeming seems to recognize no bound
or limit.   The time has come when you must unite in self defense, not
against a foreign tyrant and his armies and hirelings this time, but
against your own pretended, but treacherous fellow countrymen, who in
many respects are more dangerous and sordid.   In this contest however,
you need no weapons of offence or defense, there cannot or must not be
any indications even of violence on your part.   In the effort we have
met to consider no army can oppose you, no right minded man can but
respect it.   No one can truthfully tell you that you must hang together
or hang separately, as Benjamin Franklin told us "you have everything
to gain and nothing to lose."   Even should you fail at first you will with
additional experience and renewed courage try it again, for it would be
the height of folly to surrender or submit to defeat in a contest where
all the law, facts, justice and nine-tenths of the strength and numbers
are on your side.   How will you commence and proceed.   Have any of
you anything to offer. (A pause.)   And one arises and says: I am so

thoroughly convinced and anxious to get down to work that any suggestions from me would be a waste of time. I have been a Republican, he continued, and worked faithfully for the party since it started, but I have now laid party down forever, and here pledge myself to the faithful support of this cause. As how to proceed I am not the one to say, I am here to faithfully obey instructions. If I had been enfeebled by disease for a long time and under the treatment of a number of quack doctors of different schools who were charging me excessive and unnecessary bills, I should continue to decline in health and means until I became an impoverished invalid and about this time a physician came along who, in the most plain and convincing manner described first, the causes that originally gave me health and strength, then the causes that produced my disease with every sympton, feeling and effect, and then as plainly demonstrated to me what abomniable stuff those quack had been giving me as a remedy, and that it only aggravated the disease, and then without money and without price, he asks as a favor to give simple directions easily followed, which if complied with would restore my health and fortune. Certainly if I did not willingly and thankfully accept such an offer, no one who knew it could have any sympathy for me if I died in the poor-house or charity hospitable. This illustrates as best as. I can how I feel towards you, our benefactor and best friend. God bless you this is all I have to say. The old patriot was pleased, a smile lit up his usually grave countenance and he said: I thank you my friend for the intelligence and appreciation you manifest. I cannot understand why such men have not taken this matter in hard before this, but please remember that compliments and praise is wasted on me. Now let me hear from others who have any suggestions to offer. Here another arose and said: Every man in the room except himself perhaps could express an intelligent opinion on this matter, but said he, we are all of one mind and in order to expedite matters, we had previously agreed to have the gentleman first up speak for us all, and I ask all who feel thus to arise. Every man was instantly on his feet. Be seated gentlemen, said the old patriot, that is sufficient and satisfies me that the work so far as I can render any assistance is virtually done. All that remains is to suggest and agree upon a uniform plan of operations; as to changes to be made and work to be done, always bearing in mind that intelligence and a just appreciation of your rights and a vigilent watchfulness for their protection, and at the same time a decent regard for the rights of others is the best safeguard of the principles you are about to organize, to reestablish and knowing as I do and as you do that there is a large number of voters engaged in farming in a crude way, and as laborers all over the country, who are, unfortunately for themselves and for us, hardly pre-

paired to practically comply with this requirement. Steps must be taken
to improve their condition in this respect as well, and in a practical and
effective way, or else in time the right of franchise must be restricted to
those who are appreciative enough to at least try to use it as we intended
However much we may desire that all men everywhere could be free,
our patience is well nigh exhausted when we find that some use the right
that freedom brings to the detriment of the very principles that secures
them such rights, and to their own and other citizens detriment as well.
Some we have found who seem to persist in and act as if they liked to be
duped by schemers and sometimes even sell such a privilege for a mess
of pottage, and when such rights are made articles of merchandise for
any consideration, and good citizens tolerate such shameful acts, what I
ask can you reasonably expect as a result.   Those who are well disposed
but otherwise disqualified to comply with these requisites, you must for
the present try to aid and use all honorable means to prevent their prejudice or whims being played upon your by wily adversaries.   The first
thing to be done then is to organize and let every organization commence
right at home.   Dispose of these self constituted political bosses I alluded
to last evening, and thus make it quite unnecessary for these fellows who
are so anxious to serve you in office, to run around the country to consult
little bosses, and among you with their deceitful twaddle, about the political outlook, etc.   Do this effectively and thoroughly, and when so
done you already have reason to be thankful to each other.

   Now determine that as you have put a final veto on the man hunting
office, that those needing such offices had better look up the material to
make such a one as they want, and make this a rule of action in all your
selections for work to be done in your organizations as well.   This is one
of the most essential precautions, and is not based so much on the belief
in the scarcity of suitable and reliable men as on the general tendency of
those who are neither to crowd themselves forward to obtain positions
they are unworthy of and disqualified to fill.

   After you become organized in order to carry out this method, select a
suitable committee of investigation, a sufficient time before election,
whose duty it will be to select and reccommend men to serve you in
office.   Then your organization can select one from those thus reccom-
mended, and other things being equal those not here-to-fore conspicious
in politics must have preference.   Now when your man is thus selected,
the precautions used should be proportionate, to the trust or responsibility to be assumed.   If for some high office and especially a state or national legislator, notify the one thus selected of the facts and if he accepts
let him appear before the committees of the several organizations that
conjointly selected him and let them tell him plainly why you selected,

him, just what you want and what you expect him to do. Let there be no fooling in this matter. You have selected him and your organization is confiding in you and your judgement, and good name is to some extent at least staked on the results, and trifling does not promote confidence· You are about to place confidence in this man if you elect him, and you pay him liberally for his time, hence feel no delicacy in being plain and candid with him. He will prize your confidence more. Tell him even that means will be instituted to find out just what he will do and that in addition to liberal pay for his services, his constituents, thanks, confidence and respect will be his, if he is zealous faithful and effective, but if otherwise it can no longer be tolerated. Are you willing Sir, to accept our best efforts to elect you to represent us in congress, for example, on these conditions. Now if he is the man you want, he will gladly incourage such earnest work and freely reply something like this: I am willing to serve you to the best of my ability, if elected. Your interests are my interests, and I here promise that if at any time during my term of office, you have just cause to become dissatisfied with my acts, that I will instantly resign, and my pay as such officer ceases when notified by any authorized member of these committees to that effect, and continue faithful to the organization after. as before my election. This latter clause will seem to some impracticable, but bear in mind that such a resignation must of itself be considered an evidence of manhood and honor. Many good and true men, and able men too. might be sent to your congress, who after being there awhile might have good reasons for concluding that they happened to lack some peculiar tact or courage necessary to institute successful offensive operations in such a stronghold of wealth and ability. In such a case resignation must commend them for other positions of trust suited to their ability, taste and aspirations. Remember that if those you have been sending there were thus true to your interests, very few of them would have remained the second week.

Have as few rules as possible and respect what you do have. Avoid formality and ceremony in taking in members, and substitute alacrity and common sense. If your treasury gets full dont waste it in gew-gaws or extravagant jolifications, better remember the needy in a substantial way, it will have a better effect, and there is much more danger of having jolifications to soon, than not at all. Let all who do not understand such, at once learn simple parlimentary rules so necessary in business meetings. Many details of course will be necessary and useful. Your own good sense will be sufficient guide here.

In judging of men, no man should be suspicioned of purely selfish motives for simply desiring an office, but his actions and efforts to obtain it may fully justify such suspicion. And now in conclusion. when you begin to make your power felt, be careful about going to the other extreme. It will be just as necessary to accept prosperity or success, meekly and thankfully, as to shun adversity. Should you gain a victory common decency demands that you show respect for the feelings of the defeated. In this respect some of your political jolifications are disgusting affairs, not only for this reason, but also because the fools who yell themselves hoarse, are no better off, than if the other side were victorious. Beware of smooth tongued deceivers and adhere to the rule—Pick your man. Remember to, that many good men who join you, will be hooted at perhaps by the dirt throwers in the old parties. Your good sense must restrain from being either to confiding or to suspicious of motives, but select your men, and don't forget that right at home, in your own towns, townships and county, there is plenty of your money recklessly squandered to furnish you profitable employment between times. Have a committee to investigate where the 1 or $200,000 goes to, you tax payers pay into your county treasury every year, and find who pays the most according to their means. Look up the cost of holding your elections, especially in your unincorporated towns and public expense in general, and make an estimate of what you get for all this enormous outlay, and then when your mind reverts to original causes, you will likely think of your honorable law makers. It costs so much to elect, to legalize much of such fraud you will find some honest and reliable official, whose line of duty enables them to see much of this corruption, who will be glad to help expose such public robbery, when the people, their rightful masters, make such demand. Do this and then in purging your state and nation, you will have a multitude of willing assistants, and if by this time you do not feel like kicking yourself for having submitted to such frauds so long, you are not the Americans I take you to be, and the fact that it is your bounded duty and unqusstionable right to do so, you ought to esteem a glorious privilege.

Wake up then and make yourselves happy in the consciousness of how much you have to do, and that being done will so much increase your income and lessen your expense, and more than all, secure you happy homes and bring due respect for the rights and avocation of American producers and laborers, that others will be bound to respect. Now I am done and submit what I suggest for your correction and approval. A pause. Then the member first up arises and said: Let all present in favor of accepting every word and of adopting every suggestion here made by our best friend, and who stand ready to pledge all they posess of finanical, social or moral value, in furtherance of these ends, arise. Every man was instantly on his feet. That is sufficient said the old patriot, there is no need of any pledge, more than you show in your actions and faces. Ring the bell. This command was promptly obeyed

by Observer, and as the significant sounds pealed forth on the bright
morning air, the scenes outside cannot be described. By this time the
gathering there had increased to a multitude. and there was not perhaps
a dry eye in all that vast assembly. All wept for joy. And as the old man
modestly decended from the building, blessings were showered upon
him, and after he and Observer had spent some time in private consultation, he was again entreated to occupy his seat on the stand, so all could
see him. He consented, but said I must soon go and, after ascending
the stand with Observer and associates. he at once stepped forward and
in a clear firm voice said: My friends, my mission is fulfilled and my
hour for departure is near at hand, and I feel grateful to those in council with me, and to you, to be enabled to say that the future of our country
looks brighter now, if those in council prove to be vigilant and faithful
to their promise, and I believe that they will. and their fellow citizens in
the same avocation are even reasonably true to them. I will be permitted to visit you again, but (a pause) but if misfortune can possibly prove
so inconsistant and relentless against the wronged and needy as to cause
my advice and appeals to be remembered only in theory. we can but hope
to forget you and the opportunities you once had. I notice you call this
your country, and it is right you should. You speak with some pride of
your rights as Americans too, and it is right you should, but has it ever
occurred to you that this country and these rights are yours. to preserve.
protect and defend, and transmit. unimpared or improved to your children and posterity, but not yours to destroy, sell or neglect. Please
remember this, and remember also that the changes I have suggested
and that your council have adopted. is not of themselves any guarantee
of your success. They are but the means that when faithfully used will
accomplish this end, and so with any plan or suggestion that can be
adopted. Vigilance and common sense. at least in an ordinary degree.
is still essential to carry such plans or suggestions into practical effect.
When you people become trustful of others. and by your votes or otherwise place power in their hands, you thereby enable those thus confided
in to benefit you more or injure you more, as they feel disposed or may
be influenced, than they otherwise could, and in proportion to the nature
or extent of the power so intrusted. This being true, you should begin
to estimate more clearly the vast difference to your interests. in having
an able and faithful man, who is true to your interests, and a smooth
tounged deceitful Judas, who will sell to the highest bidder the rights
and your interest you send him to protect. Let no one among you allow
himself to conclude, and especially in politics, that what is everybody's
business, is nobody's, and that he can stand a public fraud as long as
others can, or because the loss or expense to him individually is only a

mere trifle. This kind of logic, if adhered to, would in time only relieve you of what (in this way of expressing it), you seem to consider the trouble of looking after your own best interests, but you would wake up some fine morning and find some arrogant overbearing official, looking after it for you, who would not show the least disposition to consult you as to how or when it was to be done, or how much it would cost or discommode you. I beg of you to think of these matters and act accordingly and promptly.

My true and faithful friend, Observer, will be as true and faithful to you when I am gone. Heed his council and all will be well. And now with a fervent hope for your welfare. I bid you all farewell. With a wave of the hand and moistened eyes, the old man now dissapeared among his associates. All arose and moved towards the stand for a last look at their benefactor, but the report was soon circulated that he could not be found. This was at first discredited and those who attended the council determined to find him now, and after failing to do so, went to Observer and were amazed to find him sobbing with grief at the sudden departure of his friend, and in response to their anxious enquiries, his only reply was he has gone. Never was there an assembly in whose faces the emotions of joy, sorrow and surprise were so plainly and so affectingly blended.

After the anguish caused by their friends sudden and unexpected exit had sufficiently subsided, Observer naturally became the center of attraction and was earnestly called for. He arose and said: His feelings were such as to require all the effort he was capable of making to attend to his part of this strange and affecting program. The unexpected arrival and departure, said he. of my mysterious and now absent friend here in your midst, and the unanimity and alacrity that our citizens in council with him appreciated and adopted his suggestions, constitute a wonderful and glorious coincidence, and one that will lead to a better appreciation of good men. and cause rascals to become more conspicious and culpable, and all there is left for us to do, is to be vigilant and faithful as we can to the great inducements held out to us. Let us be considerate too and not allow our ardor to carry us too far. Education and persuasion is the only means at our disposal productive of good results, and with energy and courage of our convictions. is all we need. The farmers and laboring men of this country have long and amply demonstrated their ability to bear imposition and adversity, and ought to be able now to bear a little fair play and prosperity as meekly. However well convinced and desirous for this change those of us who have witnessed this impressive revival may be. it must not be forgotten that others have an equal right to decide for themselves, and if in looking forward to results, any of our fellow citizens in poor or moderate circumstances, cannot see sufficient inducements to join our cause, we can but deplore such misfortune and fight their battles for them.

I have not been endowed with any special rights or power in this matter, the way is open and free to all citizens alike, irrespective of sex or nationality, and I earnestly entreat all such all over this broad land to organize at once and enlist in this army of peace, to meet capital at the polls and there decide whether or not laboring men and their depending families have any rights that unscrupulous shylocks, wielding capital as scourge, will be compelled to respect.

The principles that so urgently demand our attention may be considered peculiarly American, and hence the name Americans would seem appropriate for our members. But we will not be particular about this, unity of action is of first importance, and if there is a name, that more than any other will tend to neutralize old party whims and prejudice, and be more likely to induce all other industrial organizations to promptly unite with us in casting votes for mutual benefit and protection, that's the one for us. And now with no feeling of vindictiveness or desire to in any way injure those who choose to criticise or oppose us, let us press forward in the right and in the way that we believe will ultimately result in good to all.